DEATH DISTURBED

By
Lucinda E Johnson

Books by Lucinda E Johnson:

Real in the Dark
Real in the Dawn
Real in the Dead
Real in the Scare
Once Feared
Once Mortal
Once out of Range
Once Before
Down and Dead
Down then Gone
Down and Found
Death in Secret
Death out of Focus
Death Disturbed

DEATH DISTURBED

A Novel

The fourteenth Charlie Black novel

By

Lucinda E Johnson

DEATH DISTURBED

PRUGGUS PUBLISHING, LLC

Paper Book ISBN: #978-1-7325779-8-5

E-Book ISBN: #978-1-7325779-9-2

Cover design and book layout
Hoodie Beitz, Custom Graphics, Inc.
www.customgrfx@aol.com

First Printing January 2022
Printed in USA

For Pruggus, the one you can always count on.

Acknowledgments

Thanks to my friends and family real and imaginary.
Special thanks to Caroline and Sally W. Dog.
Always.
I couldn't do it without you all.

Thank you Burkie. You are the best.

CHAPTER 1

He stood at the bathroom window looking out to the woods behind his home. The inky black shadows seemed to brighten the moonlight on the snow. What did he see darting between trees? Probably nothing. Easy to imagine things in the middle of the night. What if he wasn't imagining? Maybe something really was out there tonight.

He stayed at the window long enough for the tile floor to chill his feet. He decided to make sure everything outside was all right. Without turning on any lights in the house, he retrieved his boots from the bedroom, grabbed his coat from a kitchen chair and stepped outside.

The icy night air caught in his throat. He coughed. At the very moment he coughed, he was sure he heard a noise in the trees. Was it snow crunching under an intruder's feet? Was it an animal? A coyote? A bear? A cougar? Was it snowpack falling from the branches? He was sure he heard something. He stood still. He listened and watched.

The night was clear. The moon was almost full with an icy, faintly colorful crystal ring around it. He was getting colder each second he stood there. He had to move. He walked slowly across his deck and stopped at the railing. He stared into the unnervingly dark forest. He heard something again. It was definitely snow crunching.

He thought he saw movement again. A dark shape, a shadow, a figure, moving swiftly, easily within the trees. What to do? Should he call out? Should he get his shotgun and investigate? Why would anyone or anything be skulking around on his property? In the middle of the night? In the cold? There should be a Covid-driven ten o'clock curfew in Angel Fire like the curfew they'd imposed over in Taos last spring. He didn't think the curfew would really do a lot to stem the rise of new cases of the virus. However, it might make life less stressful in some way. The pandemic put everyone on edge somehow. He felt it.

Then it occurred to him, when had he last detected movement out there? At night? When was that? He remembered. It was last month on the night of the full moon. He remembered well. He saw the shape that night, up close, clearly. It actually took a step up onto the deck. He watched it for maybe five minutes. It crouched down by the railing and stayed there in the broken shadows of the slats. No snow that night. It hadn't been as bright as tonight. Tonight the snow glowed.

That night, he had called out to the dark shape. He asked what it wanted. In reply, it had sent his soul spinning. It propelled him into the distant cold darkness of the universe, twirling silently among the sparkling yet indifferent stars. He worried. What was he doing out there? What is the universe? How does it exist? Why? Where did it come from? Didn't it have to have come from somewhere at some time? Where did he come from? Why was he there? He worried that he'd have to stay out there, always worrying. But, the dark shape had sent him back. Back to his home.

This night, he didn't feel at all safe. A jagged piercing fear rose quickly in him. He returned to the kitchen. The warm air inside the house calmed him. He stood by the back door. The upper half of the door was an uncovered window. He stood in his dark kitchen and watched the woods and his deck through that window. He thought about the danger. He knew he had to do something about it. But, tonight was not the right time.

He'd not make the same mistake this time. He couldn't bear any more stress. He did not speak. He tried to keep his thoughts from communicating with the shape. He concentrated on the mundane aspects of his day-to-day life. He knew he had to keep his mental footing sure and firmly planted. He couldn't slip. He couldn't let it get him. Even for a minute, not again. Not like last time. Please.

CHAPTER 2

As soon as Susan Mileser unlocked the office door she knew who'd been there. His ghastly smell always lingered long after he'd gone. Despite the frigid air outside, she left the door open and immediately turned on the HVAC system fan. His unmistakable aroma reliably assaulted with an astringent mix of perhaps sweat, old coffee, sour milk, and red wine. It was terribly unpleasant, and she thought, just plain nasty. She was so glad the office had a good ventilation system. If it wasn't Steve's stink, it was the evidence of a skunk's nocturnal trek under the trailer, or the smelly remains of someone's old tuna sandwich in the trash that required the powerful air flush of the HVAC.

Frustini's Design and Construction housed its office in a luxurious doublewide trailer, which at first glance, might have looked portable. But the tall pines snuggled close to the structure confirmed that it hadn't moved since it was placed on the lot twenty some years ago. Construction companies sometimes have portable offices that can be moved to and from building sites if necessary. James Frustini and his wife Susan Mileser designed and built homes in the mountains, in the forested mountains of northern New Mexico. No way to move an office to their build sites.

Most of the residential build sites were on steep and

rugged lots in the mountains surrounding the small high altitude town of Angel Fire, New Mexico. Frustini was especially busy with residential new-builds and remodels an unforeseen consequence of the Covid-19 pandemic. The unprecedented and unsettling nearly global-wide lockdown seen in the spring and early summer of 2020, along with the pervasive struggle to avoid contamination from the invisible enemy, the Covid virus, had catapulted an exodus from America's large cities. Frustini's current clientele came from California and from as far away as the east coast. So many people were now fleeing from the densely populated areas to the perceived pastoral seclusion and safety of the mountains.

Susan Mileser, the pretty, late-middle-aged co-owner of the company, sat at her desk and stared out the window nearly mesmerized by the snow dreamily falling over the town and mountains. She had a wonderful view of the ski area that swept down towards the village of Angel Fire. She watched the ski lift carrying a few brightly colored skiers up the slopes. A weekday morning in early January is historically not a very busy ski time in any year. This year the resort was open on a limited occupancy basis due to Covid restrictions. This morning seemed especially quiet. Her reverie was interrupted by the melodic chiming of her cell phone. She looked at the screen and saw it was Kako Williams calling.

"Hey. Good morning," Susan greeted her friend.

"Hey to you. What are you doing for lunch today?" Kako asked.

"Brought a sandwich. Why? Got an idea?" Susan asked.

Kako laughed, "Sure do. Let's eat out."

"Great idea. I haven't eaten out in ages. What's open? Where can we go?"

"Not a lot, but a few places have outdoor seating, even

though of course outdoor seating is restricted as per Covid mandates."

"Have you looked outside? It's about twenty degrees and snowing. That'll restrict seating," Susan explained.

Laughing, Kako said, "The pizza place has outdoor service under cover of their porch. They have those big outdoor propane heaters."

"Okay, I could go for a salad and slice. We should go early, before the skiers descend."

"My thought exactly," Kako said. "Since the seating is very limited. How about we meet there at eleven?"

"Perfect. See you then," Susan confirmed.

As she clicked off the call, James Frustini was chased in the door by a gust of snow and cold.

Susan put her mask on, as they'd made it a habit to wear a mask if anyone else was in the office, no matter who it might be.

She greeted her husband, "Morning. Getting windy out there?"

"Kinda, a little, not real windy. Yet. Think it's gonna get bad later this afternoon," the tall, handsome, sturdy, late-middle-aged man replied as he removed his boots and coat. He put his mask on and moved towards his desk.

"Steve was here this morning, before me. He was gone when I got here. Place stunk as always. Why was he here?" Susan asked.

James sat down behind his desk and said, "I don't know. Maybe he came to get the plans for the Moonboy house. He's supposed to be building out the master closet and bath this week."

"Why in heaven's name does he smell so bad?" Susan asked.

"You always ask me that. I don't know. He always has. I don't know what he eats or doesn't eat or whatever. It's annoying as hell. If he wasn't such a good finish carpenter... Have to fumigate the sites when he's through. Pain in the ass, and expensive."

"Speaking of workers, have you found anyone? We need to get going on the Klauss house kitchen," Susan noted as she looked at the scheduling spreadsheet on her computer screen.

James answered, "Nope. With the feds and the state giving out so much free money, hard to find anyone willing to work."

"It's a weird world," Susan noted.

"Tell me. We can only work on the closed-in houses right now. Can't work outside in this weather! That means I need skilled help. If I can find someone, we can start sheet-rocking the Silverpole house. This is such a cluster. Got all this business and have to search high and low for workers!" James lamented.

Susan said, "Maybe you should throw your hiring net out further. How about Denver?"

James said, "I had that thought this morning. I'll see about that. Maybe some skilled construction people from Denver might like to flee on down here."

The office door opened and fit, sixtyish-looking man in a large winter coat and fur hat stepped in. He closed the door quickly, stomped his booted feet on the mat and took off his hat revealing a head of thick, shoulder length silver hair.

"Hi James. Hi Susan. Cold as all get out! Snow's getting thicker by the minute. What're you doing?"

James said, "Hop! Thought you'd gone to New York, to see your family. Glad you're here though. I need all kinds of help. I need sheet-rockers, carpenters, plumbers, electricians!"

Hop responded, "Well, I'm all of those but the electrician. Don't like messing with electricity. I'm up for some work. What do you have? Hey, do I need to wear a mask in here?"

Susan said, "Mask is requested, yes. How long are you staying?"

"Yeah. I'd planned to drive to upstate New York, was gonna take the whole month off. But, the pandemic hasn't released its hold on humanity. I'll visit the old folks next summer maybe. For now, I'm still here," Hop explained as he put his mask on. "And I need some work. Work that pays. I'm still trying to finish my house. Nearly done. But it hasn't paid me a dollar! Nice house to live and starve in, though!"

James and Susan laughed. Susan said, "Same old story. We can relate!"

James confirmed, "Been messing with our house for years now. Don't think it'll ever be finished. You want to throw up some sheet-rock today? Over at the Silverpole house? The rock is there, stacked inside and waiting."

"Sure. That sounds fine. As long as smelly Steve Smedley isn't there. I can't take his stink. And I don't think any kind of mask can cover that up."

"He's working at the Moonboy house this week. All alone. No one can take his stink."

Susan added, "Hop, do you know why he stinks?"

Hop replied, "No. Why?"

"I don't know. I'm asking you."

"He smells like he doesn't bathe or wash his clothes, ever. At least that's how he smells to me," Hop said.

James remarked, "He does smell like that. Maybe he's homeless. I don't have any idea where he lives. Do you?"

Hop replied, "Nope. He lives somewhere near enough to the village to do his food shopping here. I've encountered him in the market."

"Bet he's given a wide berth," Susan said.

Hop laughed, "I think so!"

James said in Steve's defense, "But he's an excellent finish carpenter. Never seen better. Jeez, if all he needs is a home with a shower and laundry, we could help him. You think he'd take offense if I asked him?"

Susan said, "I could ask him. If he gets ticked off at me, no harm done."

Hop said, "Good cop, bad cop. Good plan."

"Ok. Next time he comes in, Susan, you ask him. If he takes us up on the offer, he can stay in one of our rentals, one of the condos. Pandemic driven vacancies abound right now," James suggested.

"Hope to all-that-is-clean that he takes you up on the offer," Hop said. "Gimme the key to Silverpole and I'll go rock it!"

"Great. Start with the bedrooms and hall to the main area," James instructed. "Here's a copy of the plans and a key. As a bonus, the heat is on and working. Just turn it down when you leave."

"Will do. Say, Susan, where's that handsome Herbie?" Hop asked.

"He's home. It was too cold for him. I took him out for a walk this morning and it was all he could do to stay out long enough to pee. He's not as young as he once was. Last saw him curled up in front of the woodstove."

James added, "When I left he was watching cartoons. But still in front of the woodstove."

"Tell him I asked about him. He's one of the best dogs I know," Hop said smiling.

"He is the very best!" Susan affirmed.

CHAPTER 3

Long after the cloud-dimmed light of the afternoon had faded, Hop returned to Frustini's office. James was still there, though Susan had gone home.

James asked, "You rocked the entire house, didn't you? I knew you could do it."

Hop laughed and said, "Not quite, man. I did get as far as the end of the hallway. It went pretty fast. When I don't have to work around others, I can get stuff done."

James offered him a beer or a soda. Hop took the beer and sat by the woodstove in the office. James joined him.

James asked, "How does Silverpole look?"

Hop replied, "Looks very nice. That's an interesting floor plan. Unusual layout. The views are magnificent. Can see across the valley and on to Colorado."

"What's unusual about the layout?" James asked. "It's just like other homes we've built."

"It's unusual in my experience, then. The front entrance comes right into the kitchen area. That's different for me."

"Oh, that's a current fad. The California people especially like that."

"Ah. California people. Now I get it. Say, Greg Moranos came by the site today. Is he working for you?" Hop remarked.

"Yes and no. He comes and goes. He does some

plumbing work. Pretty good plumber. Efficient."

"Did he plumb Silverpole?"

"Yes. Is it leaking??" James asked.

"No no. He poked around the kitchen and the bathrooms. Said he was looking for his wool hat. He seemed nervous and a little jumpy. Is he ok?" Hop asked.

"Well I know he has some issues, but he's ok. When he's not ok, he stays away. Sometimes it's a hardship for my scheduling, but it's alright. He's a good guy, I think," James explained.

"Does he still live up on that ridge?"

"As far as I know he does. He has about twenty acres up there. Steep terrain. Dense forest. No close neighbor was his goal, as I remember. We built his house for him. That was at least fifteen years ago. It's isolated up there, but that's what he likes. The trees make it seem even more isolated."

"He still married to Kako Williams?"

"Well, kind of. Susan and Kako are friends, so I know from Susan that Kako doesn't live with Greg, but I'm pretty sure they're still married."

"Where does Kako live?" Hop asked.

"She lives near the country club lake. She's renting a house over there."

Hop asked, "She still working? She still have that antique store?"

James replied, "She's trying to. The pandemic has changed the way so many people do business. The lockdown last spring was the beginning of the end for the usual tourism and many brick and mortar businesses. She does most all of her business online now. She says its going better than she thought it would."

Hop said, "Glad to hear it. She's a nice person. Smart,

beautiful, and energetic, though I have to admit she's too opinionated for me."

James said, "Yeah, Kako's smart. And I know what you mean about her opinions. She seems awfully judgmental. Strange that she stays married to Greg."

"How so?"

"I think it'd be tough to be legally tied to him. He's a bit off-kilter sometimes. He lives in his own world."

Hop laughed and said, "What does that mean?! Everyone in this place lives in their own world. That's why they're here! If Greg is more exaggerated than most, he is definitely special material."

James laughed, too. "He's okay, but he is special material. He has told me about some of his experiences. Aliens, and such."

Hop said, "Oh, that. Who around here hasn't had alien-ish experiences? We live at eight and a half thousand feet and above! Very close to the stars. We see more in the sky than low-landers do."

"No. I mean Greg has had close personal encounters with unknowns. He told me he didn't know if the entities were alien or spirits. Or some of each."

"Oh. Well I hope he's keeping a video journal. Could make some money from something like that."

James said, "He has a podcast."

Hop remarked, "Podcast? That's just an audio format, isn't it? He needs pictures and videos, too! Maybe interviews with the entities!"

They got another beer and remained by the woodstove talking until Susan called.

James said to Hop, "Gotta get home. Susan says I'm fixing dinner tonight. I think I'm serving spaghetti. You want to come?"

Hop accepted the invitation.

James made a fine dinner of spaghetti and grilled cauliflower. After dinner the three sat by the woodstove and had coffee and cookies.

Hop asked James, "You make these cookies?"

James replied, "Susan did. She's a cookie master."

"Sure is. These are very very nice. I don't get homemade cookies too often," Hop said.

Susan told him, "You know, cookies are not hard to make. If you can hang rock, you can make cookies."

James laughed, "So you say. I've tried, Hop, and I can tell you it takes skill and practice."

Hop asked Susan, "He talking about hanging rock or making cookies?"

"Both!" Susan replied.

"You see Kako lately?" he asked Susan.

"Yep. Saw her at lunch today. Why?"

"How is she? Beautiful as ever? Saw Greg today. He stopped by the build site Asked James about him. Just wondering how those two are. Don't see people anymore. Pandemic, you know. James told me Greg is mostly staying close to home. He okay?" Hop inquired.

Susan replied, "Kako is fine. Yes still the stunning beauty. She's as intense as always, but fine, I guess. I'm sure James told you she doesn't live with Greg anymore. Hasn't in a few years now. She says it's easier for them both, living apart. She is completely into her online store. Doing pretty well. Everyone stays home so much more these days, what with few places to go. Covid has changed everything."

Hop said, "Yes. It sure has. Even I have discovered the magic of ordering online."

James added, "The supply chains have been brutalized by Covid shut-downs. The price of materials, wood especially, has skyrocketed. And the wait times are crazy long."

Hop suggested, "Maybe the costs are inflated by Covid shut downs, but also by greedy wholesalers."

"Probably. Humans are known for their greed."

Hop laughed and asked, "Is Greg still guiding?"

Susan answered, "Yes, some. Kako said he's had some good lion hunts this fall. She went on one of them with him and his group."

Hop asked her, "Did she get a lion?"

Susan replied, "She didn't, but one of the hunters did. A big one."

Hop asked, "Where do his clients come from and where is he guiding these days?"

She said, "I understand most of his hunters are coming out of Texas and Kansas. He still goes up to Timberlake Ranch, you know, up above and past Ocate. He's had the leases up there for maybe twenty years now. Knows the place like the back of his hand. Can hunt, elk, deer, lion, bear, most any big game up there. It's a huge place. Better than fifty thousand acres."

"Who owns that ranch?"

James answered, "A trust. The trust was setup by the family of the big cosmetic company, Flowerdale. The old guard are all dead and gone. But the trust lives on for the benefit of the heirs."

Hop said, "And Greg. He's had that hunting business going as long as I've known him."

Susan said, "Yes, he's done very well with that. And has the podcast, too, these days."

James told her, "Yeah, I told Hop about that."

"But you weren't specific about the topics being cast on the pod. What does he talk about?" Hop asked.

Susan replied, "He talks about any and everything. I'm sure James told you that Greg is still a bit eccentrically off-center. He time-travels, experiences alien visitations, has on-going paranormal encounters with whomever. So his podcast topics range from plumbing tips to wormholes and hauntings."

Hop said, "Man! That should be a very popular podcast."

"It is."

Hop laughed. "Is he off-center or just well-rounded?"

"Good point!" James exclaimed.

Susan added, "He's a nutter, but a good plumber, good hunter...and apparently not a danger to anyone."

James asked, "Does Kako believe he's not dangerous?"

"Yes. She says he's just not someone to live with. I think she still loves him somehow," Susan explained. "She does see him some. She checks up on him. She goes up to his place and takes or makes dinner for him every so often. And she still hunts occasionally"

"He doesn't come to her house?" Hop asked.

"No. She doesn't let him. She says it's best that way. Seems they have established some ground rules for their situation," Susan said.

"Rules are good," Hop said. "As long as everyone follows them."

James added, "And if the rules make sense for the majority."

"Where's Herbie tonight? Haven't seen him since before dinner," Hop asked.

Susan explained, "After he growled at you... And that

was unexpected. He just doesn't growl at friends. I took him upstairs. He's sleeping on our bed."

James said, "I don't know why he growled at you like that. He must have been feeling a little off tonight. He makes his own rules."

CHAPTER 4

For several weeks, the winter weather in Angel Fire vacillated between true winter cold and snow and almost balmy daytime conditions with below zero degree freezing cold nights. By the end of January, the snow was not as deep as the resort town would have liked, but was still quite ski-worthy. Covid cases were predictably spiking nationwide as a result of the ill-advised holiday travel, and the short-sighted behavior of those who chose to engage in mask-less get-togethers. So, the resort town in northern New Mexico was quieter than most mid-winter times in years past. The future of social culture in general was still an uneasy unknown.

James Frustini was in his office, on the phone, when Greg Moranos burst in the door. James said to him, "Hey, Greg, hold on a sec. Be right with you."

Greg stomped his feet on the mat at the door. His boots were wet and muddy. He took off his coat and wool hat and hung them over a chair in front of James' desk. He sat down in the other chair, put on his mask, and stared at James.

"Ok. Call me when you have an ETA on the flooring. Thanks. I know it's out of your hands. I appreciate it. Thanks," James said into the phone before he hung up. "So, Greg, what's up?"

Greg said, "I finished the plumbing at that house you

sent me to."

"Great. The Moonboy house. So all the plumbing is in?" James asked.

"Yes. I just told you that. But it smells like there is something dead in the walls or under it. Just so you know it isn't the septic or anything to do with the plumbing," Greg stated.

James laughed. "I know the smell has nothing to do with you or your work. Steve Smedley was working there for a couple of weeks before you went in. Sorry about that."

"What is wrong with Steve? He's been stinking like that forever. I think he has some metabolic disorder," Greg said.

"Could be. Do you know where he lives?"

Greg replied, "I think he's roughing it up in the woods somewhere off to the west of my place. He's an outdoor guy."

"By roughing it, do you mean he's camping or something? In the winter?" James asked.

"I think so. Somebody told me that a couple of years ago. Said Steve lives off-the-grid," Greg explained.

"Maybe that's why he smells so bad. No running water maybe. Can't clean up," James suggested.

"Could be. But why wouldn't he go somewhere periodically and bathe and clean his clothes?" Greg asked.

"Who knows? He probably can't smell himself at all," James suggested.

"No telling what kind of diseases have attached to him. Wonder if he's had a Covid vaccination?" Greg questioned.

"He told me he had. But people lie," James said. "No one works around him so I don't think he is passing on any coodies of anything."

Greg laughed. "I hope not. I make all my hunting clients bring proof of vaccination and have negative Covid test results no more than three days old. Still they have to mask up and keep strict social distance. I don't want to be part of any super spread."

James asked, 'How many hunters do you have on a hunt?"

Greg answered, "From one to four. Sometimes a few more if there is a good reason, like a family or something. Most hunts are less than four."

"Have you had a busy fall and winter season?"

"Yes. Slows down for Christmas and New Year's, then it picks back up. This plumbing job came at just the right time for me."

"Good. Let me know when you are free again," James said.

"Hah. I'm never free!" Greg said.

"Tell me! Plumbers are a premium trade. So, what else is going on in your world? Did you have a good Christmas?" James asked.

"Christmas was fine. Kako and I had dinner up at my place. She cooked it all. Was very good. She's going with me on the next hunt."

"Oh. Cool. Does she go very often?"

"Every once in a while. She likes to hunt. She's a crack shot with gun and bow."

James asked, "Do you take the hunters on day hunts or overnights? Where do you house them?"

Greg said, "There's a very nice big house at Timberlake Ranch. The Flowerdale family built it years ago for their own use. But after the old folks died, old Mr. and Mrs. Flowerdale, the younger ones quit coming out here. They've been trying to bust the trust for the past few years. They want to sell the ranch. But the trust is ironclad. I guess the constant stream of money from all of those cosmetic sales just isn't enough for those heirs.

"Anyway, I have use of the ranch house for my hunters. It's quite nice. I hire a couple from Mora who care-take the place when hunters are there. You know, clean and cook and such. The hunters love it."

James asked, "Do you take them hunting by horseback?"

"Oh no, I have off-road vehicles and trucks. Horses would be an additional cost and concern that I don't want," Greg explained.

"How's your podcast going?" James asked.

"Just great. Have such an interesting and loyal following. And I enjoy doing the podcasts!"

"Topics?" James posed.

"Same old same old. About my life and times. I engage the listeners when appropriate. We talk about UAPs, the universe, levels of existence and dimensions, and of course plumbing," Greg replied.

"What's UAP?" James asked.

Greg smiled and said, "Oh that's the government's new terminology for what we used to refer to as UFOs. UAP is Unidentified Aerial Phenomenon. When the government decided to acknowledge that unidentified extraterrestrial visits are real, they needed a new name for them. How could they use the name UFOs that they'd so staunchly denied for so long?"

"Oh. Sure, they'd look kinda dumb to say, at this late date, that UFOs were real."

"Exactly. UFOs are not real, but now UAPs are. Typical government double-talk," Greg agreed.

Greg stood and put on his coat and hat.

James asked him, "You want your check now?"

Greg answered, "No rush. Just mail it to me. Good to see you. Tell Susan hello please."

After Greg left, James immediately called Susan to report the visit.

"Greg always seems so normal, even when he throws in the references to supernatural or any other off-beat thing. He's a good guy," James said to Susan.

She replied, "I know. He's an enigma. A nice guy with a fascinating edge to him. I've never been around him when he's off-in-space as Kako terms it. She says he's different then. I like the Greg I know."

CHAPTER 5

It was some days later, when Hop Sovern stopped by James Frustini's construction company office. He was out of breath as he stepped in the door. The day was dark with heavy low clouds making time undeterminable.

"James! Susan! Have you heard what they found?" Hop asked as he stomped the wet snow and mud from his boots, hung up his coat, and put on his mask.

"Hi Hop. What are you talking about?" James responded.

Susan was at her desk. She said, "Slow down, Hop. What's going on?"

Hop looked from one to the other and said, "What was found up at Greg Moranos' place?"

Susan said, "I don't know. Gold?"

James said, "I don't know. What?"

Hop sat down and caught his breath. He said, "Human remains. A surveyor found them. He was on foot, well snowshoe, crossing the top part of Greg's place. Greg's property runs up and down the mountain, you know. His house is on that flat area towards the bottom. The bones were up at the top part."

James said, "I know. We built his house. He has about twenty acres. Most of it runs nearly straight up the mountainside. What do you mean human remains? Bones?"

Hop said, "Just that. The surveyor said he looked down the incline from where he was and saw tombstones. He said he'd never known of a cemetery up there, so he climbed down to look at it. Not only were there tombstones, but there were bones sticking up through the dirt, rocks, and snow."

"Good God! Just the bones, no caskets?" Susan asked.

"Was it a bone-fide cemetery, or a bon-a-fide cemetery?" James asked.

Hop smiled and said, "That's funny. The weather has been so squirrely, cold, but with warmer days, that the snow has already begun to melt on the clear areas of south facing slopes. That's where this place is. South facing with trees around it, but mostly cleared. The snowmelt caused some sliding of the soil and rocks. Turned over some of the tombstones and released some of the buried."

"So, whose cemetery is it?" Susan asked. "Did Greg know it was there?"

Hop answered, "Don't know that part. The surveyor came back to town and notified Sheriff Deelly. Guess they're going to have to investigate."

"How do you know about this?" James asked.

"I heard it at the market. Just went in for bread and milk. Everyone in there was talking about it. Apparently, the surveyor stopped in after he left the Sheriff's office. He said he checked the maps of the area up there and no cemeteries were marked."

"Were the tombstones old?" Susan asked.

"I only heard that they were small tombstones. Not the large ones you usually see. And there was no writing on them. Just the stones," Hop explained.

"How small?" Susan asked.

"Don't know," Hop said.

"Could be an old settler's cemetery, or a miner's," James added.

"Yeah. Could be. But the surveyor said there were pieces of clothing that didn't look real old."

Susan said, "Clothes? On the bones?"

Hop replied, "Clothes and bones. Kinda together. Pulled out of the ground by the sliding mud and rocks."

"Jeez. Something else to worry about! First, single use plastic bags, and straws, then Covid, now this! Secretive cemeteries! What next?" Susan said laughing, shaking her head.

"UAPs," James said with a sigh.

"A what?" Hop asked.

Susan answered, "Greg said that's the new government acronym for UFOs. UAPs, Unidentified Aerial Phenomenon."

James added, "Well now we have UBP. Unidentified Buried Phenomenon."

CHAPTER 6

Sheriff's deputy Marvin McShine knocked on Greg Moranos' front door just after lunchtime. He waited in the silence of the winter mountain forest setting for what seemed to him like a long time before Greg answered the door.

"Hi Marvin. Guess you're here about the graves?" Greg said.

Deputy McShine said, "Yes. Can you take me up to the site?"

Greg answered, "Sure. It's a rough hike. Let's take the four-wheelers"

"Even though it is such a gorgeous sunny winter day, I was hoping you'd suggest that. The surveyor reported it was way up the mountain."

"Yeah, Artie told me all about what he saw up there. I think we can find it with no problem," Greg said.

It was a slow slippery serpentine ride up the steep rocky, muddy, and snowy trail. After many switchbacks, they were close to the cleared area where the graves had been found. They left the off-road vehicles and slogged the last short way to the cleared area on the mountainside, to the cemetery.

On seeing the tombstones, Marvin remarked, "God. Greg, did you know this was here?"

Greg replied, "Not until Artie found them. I don't come

up here. Don't think I've been up here to this particular spot in years."

Marvin asked, "You don't walk your land?"

"No. I don't have time to hike for fun. I work a lot. Have to scout the Timberlake Ranch for the hunts. That's enough hiking for me."

"What was Artie doing up here?" Marvin asked.

Greg replied, "He was surveying the land above mine. This is almost at the top of my parcel. He said he came down here as he was crossing though this skinny part of my place. From here, and then east, southeast, and down, my plat sort of widens out into a rectilinear shape the rest of the way down to my house. My house sits near the bottom, southern border of my land."

"So this area is yours, and is surrounded on three sides by your neighbors but is attached to your property. A peninsula sorta?"

Greg affirmed, "Correct."

Marvin noted, "So, easy access to this site from other people's property? How close are we to your neighbors?"

"Not real close. Maybe there's at least a half-acre or more buffer on all three sides from where we are now. I'll show you the map when we get back to the house."

Marvin used his cell phone to photograph the graves as he carefully walked the perimeter of the site. Greg just watched.

Marvin called to Greg from across the cemetery, "Greg, come look at this."

"Jeez. What in the world?" Greg said as he saw what Marvin was pointing at.

On the ground by one of the toppled tombstones was an obviously old and weathered unopened snack-size package of corn chips and a mud-encrusted cell phone.

Marvin said, "Maybe kids did this."

Greg responded, "Why do you say that?"

"Well, corn chips and a cell phone..."

Greg said, "Don't be ridiculous. Everyone has corn chips and cell phones."

Marvin conceded, "Okay. So, I count twelve of these little tombstones. Look like they're less than half-size of a traditional stone."

Greg said, "Tombstones come in all sizes and shapes. I think the remarkable fact is that these are all the same size and shape, and have no inscriptions."

Marvin again conceded, "Yes. That is odd."

"This whole thing is odd. Let's find where the grim reaper accessed this area. Had to have come in from above. Too hard to get up here from below," Greg said.

Greg led Marvin north into the trees surrounding the cemetery. They continued straight up the mountainside about fifty yards. There Greg pointed out the bright pink spray painted marks around the girth of some trees.

"This is the property line of my land. See. Look this way. The pink mark is on trees that're on or nearly on the boundary. You can see the line if you look through the forest," Greg explained.

Marvin looked and said, "Kinda like a fence, but no fence. I see."

"Let's walk this line. We'll see where entry has been made."

They climbed and followed the pink marked trees around the edge of the finger shaped piece of property. On the west side, they found what they were looking for.

Greg said, "Here we go. Here is the way in. See the tire

tracks."

Marvin examined the tracks on the trail blazed possibly by a pickup truck. He took photos of the clearest of the tire tracks. The tracks came from the west and wound through the trees and terrain into Greg's property towards the cemetery.

Marvin asked, "No trail or road here before?"

Greg explained, "Well not that I'm aware of. Not supposed to be, anyway. Like I said, I haven't been up here in a very long time."

Marvin said, "Let's see where this road comes from."

They walked the makeshift slushy icy muddy dirt road until it hit a dirt logging road on the adjacent property.

Marvin asked Greg, "You know whose land this is?"

Greg said, "Not sure. Probably belongs to Craymist. He bought a lot of land up here some years ago. Maybe he's selling. Maybe that's why Artie was up here surveying. He'll know the story."

Marvin said, "Sure. Let's get back."

At Greg's house, they met the Sheriff sitting on the front steps. Sheriff Deelly said, "Hi. Hoped you'd get back soon."

Deputy Marvin McShine said, "Hey, Brad. Greg took me up to the gravesites. Weird, a very remote and hard to get to place. I have the pics you asked for."

"Let's take a look," Sheriff Brad Deelly said. "Greg, it's cold, can we go inside and get some coffee or something. You want us to mask-up to go inside."

Greg said, "Oh. If you will please. Sure, come on in. I'll make some coffee."

The two officers masked-up. They followed Greg inside. The large house was for the most part one big open space with a kitchen at one end, and a fireplace at the other end. It was nicely but sparsely furnished. They sat at the big rectangular eating table. Marvin and Brad looked at the pictures of the graves on Marvin's cell phone.

The sheriff asked Marvin, "Besides the photos, did you collect any evidence?"

Marvin answered, "No. Didn't disturb anything. I figured the state police'll send their CSI people up there."

"They can have the whole mess. With those disturbed graves, it'll be an evidence collection challenge. I suspect they'll in turn give it to the FBI. The usual passing of the messiest cases. No one really wants to deal with this kind of thing," Brad Deelly said.

Greg served the men coffee and then spread a map out on the table.

"Here's the map of my and adjacent properties. It's an old map, but my property lines are the same." Pointing to the logging road marked on his neighbor's land, Greg said, "Here's the logging road we found, Marvin. That trail or path from the cemetery runs about here."

"Okay. We'll direct the state investigators, or whoever ends up taking this case, to enter from that logging road."

Greg said, "Thanks. Really don't want any new roads made through my place. What do you think has happened up there? Is it a real cemetery? Aren't there state laws regarding where a cemetery can be established?"

Sheriff Deelly replied, "Sure there are laws. But there haven't always been. In the old days, natives, families, pioneers, miners might make a cemetery for their own people, or a small community, just about anywhere. Usually it was put on a hill with a nice view. And these days, people are apt to do any crazy old thing if they think they can get away with it."

Marvin laughed and added, "That's the truth. People!"

Greg Moranos mused, "But why would somebody pick

such a remote and inaccessible spot?"

Sheriff Deelly answered, "Probably because they're hiding something."

CHAPTER 7

The town of Angel Fire was abuzz with gossip about the cemetery that Artie Tibbet had stumbled on up in the woods. A few people, all wearing masks, were milling inside the small lobby at the sheriff's office when he and his deputy returned from Greg Moranos' house.

Deputy McShine saw the little crowd and said, "Ok now. We don't have anything to tell you. You can all go on. When we have more to share, we will."

A tall skinny man asked, "So it's really true? Moranos has been burying people up at his place?"

"No no no!" Sheriff Deelly emphasized. "Greg didn't even know it was there. Artie Tibbet stumbled on the cemetery while he was out surveying. Coulda been there a hundred years."

"But still, Greg is a bit strange," a small young woman with pink hair said.

Someone else said, "Yeah, and it's not strange to have pink hair?"

The pink-haired woman remarked, "I don't think so. Have you listened to Greg's podcasts? Those are strange."

Another woman said, "I love his podcasts."

"Maybe old Commodore Craymist did it," a man said.

"There is no evidence of any person doing anything,"

McShine assured them.

"Well somebody buried somebody," a young man insisted.

Deputy McShine said, "You folks can go on outside to talk about podcasts and pink hair. We have work to do."

The gossiping group reluctantly shuffled out of the sheriff's office. Marvin watched them as they slowly moved on towards their vehicles.

Sheriff Brad Deelly said, "If this were 1890, that group would have the makings of an ugly mob. We need to get some kind of actual investigation going. I'll call the state police right now. See what they can do."

Marvin asked, "Why not just call the FBI right off? Get them involved at the start. You know it's going to end up in their hands."

"Protocol. Don't want to hurt the feelings of the state police. You know how territorial agencies can be," the sheriff said.

"Okay. I get it."

Sheriff Deelly called the SP office in Taos and asked for assistance with the matter. He learned that two state police investigators, Toady Mills and Maddy Lucero would be assigned. They should be in Angel Fire by end of day.

Just as the evening darkness began to cloak the village of Angel Fire, Toady Mills pulled into the parking lot at the sheriff's office. Deputy McShine came out to greet him.

"Toady! Great to see you! How are you?" Marvin McShine exclaimed.

The tall, handsome, middle-aged New Mexico State Police Criminal Investigator Toady Mills got out of his marked police SUV, stretched, put his mask on, and said, "You look good! Mister masked deputy! How's everything?"

Marvin laughed and said, "We're glad you're here. This newly discovered cemetery is crazy. It is way up in the mountains. Access is basically from an old logging road, then through the forest on a trail we believe was made by whoever put the graves in there. I just saw it today."

Toady said, "That's a lot of info right off the bat. Thanks. Maddy'll be here first thing in the morning. She's bringing Scout with her. He'll help locate all the remains."

"Okay. So do you have a place to stay lined up?" Marvin asked.

"I talked to James Frustini. He said I could stay at one of his condo rentals. Seems he has vacancies."

"Good. Didn't know you know James. The pandemic has lightened the winter tourism dramatically. James and everyone have vacancies that they usually wouldn't have right now."

"Yeah. James is an old fly-fishing friend. Haven't seen him in a couple of years. He and Susan asked me to dinner tonight. But before I go, do you have a map of the area where the cemetery is? Or show me on Google?"

Marvin said, "Yes. Sure. Come on in the office. I'll tell you the little bit I know. And show you the pictures."

Sheriff Deelly put his mask on when Marvin and Toady came in. "Toady! You're looking good. Great to have you here. How's Andrew?"

"Brad, good to see you, too. Andy's fine. We haven't been to Angel Fire in ages. Have to get him up here. So, you have the case of the mysterious unexpected cemetery. Tell me about it," Toady said.

"Oh lord. Yes. Artie Tibbet, a surveyor, came upon what appears to be an unregistered cemetery up in the mountains. From the photos Marvin took today, looks like a dozen tombstones. There are bones and clothing and such that have bobbed to the surface."

Toady interrupted, "Wait. What? Bobbed to the surface? What do you mean?"

Marvin answered, "Yeah. The area where the tombstones are is really a steep cleared area. The weather has been warm during the days often enough to begin the snow melt in sunny spots like this clearing. The melt-water running down this slope has pushed mud and rocks and some of the tombstones downhill enough to unearth body parts and stuff."

"And stuff?" Toady asked.

"Greg and I saw an old bag of corn chips and a pretty toasted cell phone by one of the tombstones. Looked like they'd been buried and then were pulled to the surface by the runoff."

"Who's Greg?" Toady asked.

"Oh. Greg Moranos owns the property where the cemetery was found. He lives up there. His property consists of about twenty acres of the mountainside. His house is on a flat, more level, area at the base of the plat. The cemetery is on a pretty steep area up at the top of his land," Marvin explained.

Toady said, "Sounds like these are very shallow graves."

Sheriff Deelly said, "Must be. And the tombstones all look alike. It's not the usual old cemetery. Can't tell from the pictures if there is any age to it at all."

"We'll be able to date it. First off, with luck, the corn chip bag will have a lot number and date on it. And the cell phone might provide all sorts of info," Toady remarked.

Marvin said, "I'll print out the Google map for you and mark it. In the morning I'll take you and Maddy up to meet Greg Moranos."

"Okay thanks. I'd better head on over to James and

Susan's house. Thank you both for the help," Toady said as he prepared to go.

Brad Deelly said, "James and Susan can give you a rundown on Greg Moranos. He's an interesting character."

CHAPTER 8

The next morning, Maddy and Scout met Toady at the sheriff's office. Sheriff Brad Deelly and his deputy, Marvin McShine had coffee and pastries waiting for them.

Scout remembered both the sheriff and his deputy. And they were delighted to see Scout again.

"Hey. Here's the smartest dog in the world!" exclaimed Marvin. "I brought sausage for him. Okay to give it to him?" Marvin asked Maddy.

"Did you bring some for me, too?" Maddy asked.

Marvin laughed and replied, "You bet. Sausage in the croissants!"

"Okay, then all is well," Maddy laughed.

Toady said, "I studied the map, and I think I can find the lost but now found cemetery. Looks like we can go the same way as our unknown cemetery groundskeeper's been going in: county road, to logging road, to the blazed-trail."

Marvin agreed, "Yes. That way should be good by vehicle. But I want you to meet Greg Moranos first, since you'll be on his property at the cemetery."

"Oh, of course. We can go to Mr. Moranos' first," Toady responded. "I look forward to meeting him. James and Susan told me about him."

After enjoying the hospitality at the sheriff's office,

Toady in his state police SUV, and Maddy and Scout in her state police marked pickup truck followed Deputy Marvin McShine up to Greg Moranos' house. Greg was out front waiting for the caravan.

Toady put his mask on as he stepped from his SUV. "Hello. Mr. Moranos? I'm New Mexico State Police Criminal Investigator Torrence Mills. But please, call me Toady. And this masked state police officer is Maddy Lucero. Her partner there is Scout."

Greg responded, "Hello. Call me Greg."

Marvin said, "Greg, can we come inside. I brought you some croissants."

"Great. Oh sure. Let's go inside," Greg replied.

Inside, they sat at the dining table. Greg offered coffee, but his guests declined since they'd just had coffee and pastries. So Greg ate while they talked to him.

Toady said, "I had dinner last night with James Frustini and Susan Mileser. They told me that you are their best plumber, and that you have a podcast! How long have you been a podcaster?"

Greg answered between bites of croissant, "Launched my podcast last year. It has become a consuming hobby. It's fun to do and people seem to like it."

Maddy asked, "How often do you air?"

Greg said, "I produce a full hour podcast every week."

"What's your focus topic?" Maddy asked.

"It's an eclectic mix of plumbing tips, news of UAPs, and discussions regarding the universe and meaning of life and death. Also any paranormal events are open for inclusion."

"UAPs?" Maddy asked.

"Unidentified Aerial Phenomenon. It's replaced the acronym UFOs in the government and popular nomenclature.

The federal government now acknowledges UAPs are actual and real and some are not of this planet. Consequently they had to brand them with a new name," Greg explained.

"Yes. I've seen some footage on the news. Video evidence captured by the air force. Interesting stuff," Maddy said.

Toady asked, "What sort of paranormal activity have you had? Anything here at your home?"

Greg replied, "Oh, a good deal of paranormal activity occurs here. I think these mountains are a favorite environment for energies."

"What have you witnessed?"

"Lights and the absence of lights are frequent events. The absence of light is more disturbing than the presence of light anomalies. The absence is what I imagine a black hole might feel like. It's a heavy menacing blackness that blocks whatever is behind it," Greg explained.

"Like a very dense shadow?" Maddy asked.

"Kinda," Greg said.

Maddy added, "I think I've experience such a thing."

"Tell me about it," Greg said.

"Well it was while on a case I was involved in. I was in a barn over near Mora, at a farm where a triple homicide had occurred. Scout was with me. We were investigating, looking around inside the barn. There were no animals in the barn. When Scout froze and began a low serious growl, I looked where he was looking, into a stall. A black mass materialized out of a side wall. It expanded. I couldn't see through it at all. There was no light in it, and it had no reflective quality at all. It seemed to absorb the light and air as it expanded."

Greg asked, "What time of day was it?"

Maddy replied, "It was midday. Sunny mild fall day. The barn was very bright inside. Well except for the black mass."

"How did you feel?" Greg asked.

"I felt like I was in another world. It changed the reality of the moment. I was curious, cautiously curious."

"How did it resolve?" Greg asked.

"The dark mass undulated some and moved around in the stall. Then it appeared to be sucked back into the wall. It left a dead silence. Very weird," Maddy said.

"Jeez. Maddy. I never heard about this. How big of a thing was it?" Toady interjected.

Maddy said, "At its largest, it was about as big as you are."

"I'm six-three. That was big dark thing," Toady remarked.

"It shrunk down to about the size of my fist before it finally vanished into the wall of that horse stall," Maddy added.

Greg asked, "Did it communicate with you?"

Maddy thought about that for a second and then answered, "You know, I think it did in a way. It seemed to console me somehow. I think it was telling me that everything was alright. Though I don't know how to explain what that everything was."

"You should come on my podcast and relay the experience."

"I'd like to listen to one of your podcasts, then let you know."

"Sensible," Greg said.

Toady asked, "Did the temperature change during or after the thing manifested?"

"Not that I noticed. I was about ten feet away from it, just outside the stall, in the barn's breezeway center aisle," Maddy said. "Scout never barked. He stayed on his feet and very still. His growl was low and came and went during the episode."

Marvin spoke, "I've seen UAPs. But I've never had a face-to-face with anything. Wow."

Greg asked Marvin, "You've seen UAPs? How often? Where?"

"Over the mountains all around the Moreno Valley. I see them fairly often, day and night. So often, that they seem sorta normal now. This area of the state is ripe with sightings. We get calls all the time. Usually visitors make those calls. Locals don't bother anymore," Marvin explained.

"That's what I hear from my listeners," Greg said.

Maddy asked Greg, "Any paranormal manifestations here at your house?"

Greg answered, "Yes. Energies visit me here. Usually at night. They are outside always. They favor the deck on the back of the house."

Marvin asked, "Do they talk?"

Greg answered, "No, they don't vocalize. They do communicate. I'd describe it as telepathic communication."

"What do they communicate?" Marvin asked.

Greg said, "If I ask the energies what the universe is. They try to show me. At least I believe that is what is going on. It can be telepathically conversational in a stilted kind of way. But I have learned to be very careful what kinds of queries I make. I have to control my thoughts when faced with their communications. They seem to be quite literal in their understanding and responses."

Maddy asked, "So what is the universe?"

Greg said, "Oh they showed me. They took my spirit, my energy into the vastness of the universe. It was terrifying. My response was intense, anxious. I found I was only able to worry. I worried I'd not get back to myself. I worried my energy would be out in space in the unending universe forever and ever."

Toady said, "God! That sounds intense. Were you in a ship of any kind?"

"Oh no. It was simply my energy, loose, out there. No form or substance," Greg explained.

"But you got back," Marvin said.

"I did, but now I'm afraid I might not be so fortunate next time. My plan is not to have a next time. That's what I mean about controlling what I think when they come. I cannot wonder or request just anything. I don't want to be thrust out into the emptiness without more info, or preparation."

Toady asked, "What kind of info? From where? From whom?"

Greg replied, "I don't know. Yet. I hope that someday they'll offer some instruction or something. Being projected from this familiar planetary nest out into the incredible vastness of space, far into the openness of the universe, is completely terrifying."

Toady remarked, "I can only imagine."

Marvin said, "We're going up to the cemetery."

Greg responded, "Sure. I thought so. You want to use the four-wheelers?"

"No. Thanks though. We're going to drive up there, taking the route we believe whoever's been going up there has been taking," Toady said.

Marvin added, "The county road to the logging road to the track made by the trespassers."

Greg nodded. "I might meet you up there after a while. I'll take the off-road route. If you hear my four-wheeler, don't shoot."

CHAPTER 9

As the caravan of the three official vehicles turned off the asphalt county road onto the muddy dirt logging road, Deputy Sheriff Marvin McShine, who was in the lead, stopped. He got out and walked back to Toady's state police SUV. Maddy's pickup was right behind the SUV. She joined Marvin, at Toady's driver's side window.

Maddy asked, "Is there a problem?"

Marvin said, "Just got a call from the sheriff. Seems the owner of this adjacent land called in a complaint this morning. He said someone had been using this, his logging road, as an easement. And it is not an easement. He's posted private property, no trespassing. The signs are properly and adequately displayed. His complaint is legit."

"Yeah. I saw the signs. Let's go talk to him. Where does he live?" Toady suggested.

"I agree. Let's go see him. It's not far up the county road to his driveway. Follow me," Marvin said.

The three vehicles backed out onto the county road, then after less than a quarter mile, Marvin turned in at a modest gated entrance. The gate was open. They continued up the plowed but slippery gravel driveway as it wound through the thick forest. Marvin led them to a large plowed parking area in front of an imposing two-storied log home. An older man wearing a cowboy hat and a big wool coat was sitting in the sunlight on the edge of the veranda that spanned the front of the house. He was cleaning a rifle.

Marvin was driving a sheriff's department SUV, Toady was in his state police SUV, and Maddy was in her state police pickup. It was an official looking visit. The man on the porch stood up as the three vehicles parked and the officers approached him.

"Goodness! This is what I'd call a rapid response!" the man exclaimed. "I just called in a little while ago."

"Hi, Com. The sheriff relayed your message. We were nearby," Marvin said.

"Hi Marvin. Who'd you bring with you?" Commodore Craymist asked.

Marvin McShine replied, "Commodore Craymist, this is New Mexico State Police Criminal Investigator Torrence Mills, and State Police Officer Maddy Lucero. The handsome dog with Maddy, is Scout."

"Criminal investigator? I called in a trespassing complaint!" Com laughed.

"Commodore Craymist, we are investigating that very issue, on your neighbor's property, Greg Moranos' property," Toady said.

"Call me Com. Commodore is my given name, not a title. Little bit of humor from my parents. My father was named Senator Craymist by his parents. Amusing family tradition to make it hard on the kids," Com laughed.

"I thought Torrence was a burden! Call me Toady, please. How many acres do you have here, Com?"

"My property is a little over five thousand acres. Mostly timber. I don't know Greg Moranos well. Only know he has land east and south of me. My property skirts around a small panhandle area at the top end of his property. What kind of trespassing over at his place?" Com asked.

Deputy McShine answered, "Some one or more people apparently have been accessing that small area at the top of Greg's property by way of your logging road. They have put a cemetery there on Greg's land. We are going to check it out. We'd like to use their same entry route, your logging road."

"That logging road doesn't go all the way to Moranos' property line. It's not an easement," Com noted.

"Where your road ends, the perpetrators have made their own track through the woods from your place into Greg's. That track ends at the cemetery," Marvin explained.

"Is it an old cemetery?" Com asked.

"We don't know. We have just started the investigation," Marvin said.

Toady continued, "This is our first look at it. Marvin was up there yesterday with Greg. Artie Tibbet, the surveyor found it. He was..."

Commodore interrupted, "Artie's been working for me. Been surveying that whole eastern side of my plat. I want to get a fence put up. Too many wanderers spotted. I don't want squatters or poachers on my land."

Marvin said, "Well, Artie was crossing through Greg's place, up near where your property meets Greg's, and he found the cemetery. Neither he nor my office was able to find any cemetery marked on any maps. So, we have to investigate."

"Ok. Well get going then," Com said. "Call me if there's anything I can do. Keep me in the loop."

"Thanks. I'll report back when we know what it's all about," Marvin assured him.

The officers left Craymist's property and continued their trek to the cemetery site. At the end of the logging road, the trail made by the trespassers began. The rough trail wound around trees and up and down as forced by the mountain topography. The going was slow, but it was apparent that the interlopers had made the trail with a full sized vehicle, probably a pickup truck, rather than any kind of smaller off-road vehicle.

Finally they reached the cleared area. They parked as far back from the clearing and as far to the side of the trail as the forest allowed. Maddy immediately began pulling equipment from the back of her truck. She placed a scanning 3-D laser camera on a low tripod at the point where the trail met the clearing. She initiated the scan of the trail and cemetery.

Marvin remarked, “You guys have the best equipment! What’s that going to do?”

Maddy said, “This is going to give us a three dimensional representation of the tire impressions, footprints, and all other ground disturbances in its range.”

“Ah. No more plaster casts!”

“Correct.”

“Well some of these footprints are from Greg and me yesterday. We left our four-wheelers over there. We didn’t drive over here. Those tire tracks are not ours,” Marvin explained.

Toady was walking the perimeter of the steep cleared area of the cemetery. “Jeez, the erosion has been severe. Many of these graves are washed up. Lots of material has come to the surface. Remains and artifacts!”

Marvin joined Toady at the edge of the cemetery. “God almighty, that’s an arm and hand!”

Toady said, “With both bare bones and other relatively un-decomposed parts, I think we have a cemetery with at least a few years’ use.”

“The tombstones are devoid of names, but some do

have small numbers on them," Maddy noted as she repositioned her camera and continued cataloguing.

Toady examined the tombstones closest to where he and Marvin stood. "I see. There is a small five-digit number engraved in the curved top of some of the stones. The numbers seem to be different on each. And some stones don't have numbers."

Motioning at the tombstones, Marvin asked, "What are these made of?"

"Concrete or plaster. Looks like they were each poured in the same mold," Maddy said. "The images I'm collecting will confirm if they all really came from the same mold."

"That'd mean this is a contemporary construction rather than any historical cemetery," Marvin suggested.

"Unless it was originally put here long ago and more recently spruced up with new tombstones," Toady mused.

Maddy said, "We need to get our CSI team up here and tent this site. There is so much to document and so much evidence to preserve and collect."

Marvin asked, "How can you tent this steep of a site? Next time it rains, or warms up more, this all going to continue sliding down the mountain."

"It is a precarious location. Gravity and friction are not working with us here. I think we may need to ask for help from the FBI. They have the really cool toys!" Toady said.

Maddy agreed, "Yes. Initiate the bat-signal."

CHAPTER 10

FBI Special Agent Charlie Black, and his old friend, FBI Agent-in-Charge Jackson Avery, sat in a booth at the barbeque restaurant across the street from the FBI District Headquarters in Dallas. Other than the small staff, there were only two other people in the restaurant. The recommended restrictions spurred by the on-going spikes of Covid infections meant most restaurants had seating limitations, and were predominately doing take-out business. The two FBI agents were on a late lunch break.

Jackson's cell phone rang. He looked at it and then answered the call. He mostly listened with very little response required from him. It didn't last long. He put the phone back in his pocket.

Jackson said to Charlie, "We've got to get back to the office. Let's get this packed to-go."

Back in the conference room attached to Jackson's office, he and Charlie finished their lunch as they held a video conference call with New Mexico State Police Criminal Investigator Torrence Mills.

"Toady, what in the world is happening in New Mexico now?" Jackson asked.

"Hi Jackson. Hi Charlie. Well, it seems we have a bit of a mystery on our hands. The mystery of the unexplained cemetery.

A surveyor stumbled onto a cemetery up in the mountains in Colfax County not far from Angel Fire. The cemetery appears to be fairly recently established, though not officially established of course. The site is accessible only by trespassing at least two owners' properties. The trespassers forged their way in through some challenging forested mountain terrain to bury the bodies…" Toady began.

Charlie interrupted, "Wait, how many bodies are you talking about?"

"Multiple. There are twelve tombstones. Shallow graves. Could be more," Toady replied.

"How long has this cemetery been in use?" Jackson asked.

"We can't tell yet. So far, we've left everything as we found it. I'll upload the pictures and the 3-D scans right now."

Charlie heard his phone. He retrieved and sent the images onto the same screen of the video call. Now they could all view the pictures and scanned images in a picture-in-picture screen arrangement.

"Is the ground that steep, or are the pictures slanted?" Charlie asked.

"It's that steep. That's why the graves were disturbed. The winter has been snowy, wet, and day-time warm enough to begin a rather early ground thaw in sunny spots up in that area. The incline is acute. As the daytime thaw releases the rocks and topsoil, it all slides downhill. Then the nighttime freezing moves the debris more. That thaw and refreeze cycle with the resulting sliding debris and mud opened some of the graves and toppled tombstones. We found those twelve uniform sized tombstones. That's where the estimated body count came from. But we don't yet know if every stone lays claim to a body, or vice-versa."

"Holy moly! What next?" Charlie exclaimed examining the pictures on the screen. "Someone went to a lot of effort to get the bodies there, set the stones, but didn't bury very deep! Makes little sense so far."

Jackson said, "Well, it is New Mexico. When has there been anything but highly unusual nefarious activity there?"

"True that!" Toady agreed. "We like to keep things interesting out here!"

"So, what can we do to help?" Jackson asked Toady.

Toady laughed, "Er. Take it over. Make it your case. You have the resources to handle such a case. We really don't."

Jackson said, "It does appear it might be a serial killer's dump site. I think we can take jurisdiction. Charlie will be happy to come out there to confer."

Charlie said, "I will?"

Jackson added, "I'm sure this will be a fascinating assignment. You can call in Sam and Carlos to assist. They love climbing around on cold, muddy, snowy, mountains."

Charlie laughed, "You're sure! Okay Toady, we'll leave the paper work to Jackson. I'll meet you in Taos tomorrow evening."

Toady said, "I'm both glad and relieved that you are coming. Pack your warm FBI jacket, it is winter here."

"What is the weather there?"

"It is very cold at night and can be very cold in the day or balmy warm. It can snow or it can be clear blue sky," Toady replied.

Charlie laughed, "Ok. The weather is as the weather does."

They completed the call. Toady sent the GPS coordinates of the cemetery site, so Jackson was able to pull up the most recent satellite images of the area involved.

"That really is a remote site! You can see the clearing and even the tombstones. Jeez, what a lot of trouble to get in there. Who'd go to that much trouble?" Charlie mused.

Jackson said, "It seems kinda ritualistic maybe. The tombstones are alike. From what we can see in the pics and scans, and the satellite images, the graves seemed to be in a basically evenly spaced grid pattern of three by four. The site is super remote. I'll send a crime scene crew up there tomorrow. They'll come out of Denver, so should be there about the time you get there."

"I can fly to Taos. Maybe the Santa Fe office can get a vehicle to the Taos airport for me."

"I'll see you have a mountain-worthy vehicle waiting for you. Sam and Carlos can fly in to Taos, too. They are back in Chicago today from an assignment in Boston. They'll just have to repack for a trek to the mountains!" Jackson told him.

"Is your house in Taos available for us?" Charlie asked.

"It is. And I'll ask the property manager to stock it with a gourmet selection of groceries for you," Jackson told his dear friend.

CHAPTER 11

Charlie got home a little early. Our home in Tyler, Texas is about an hour's drive from his office in Dallas. Usual evenings see his arrival later than today's. I was in the kitchen staring into the refrigerator when he surprised me.

"What are you looking for?" he asked from the kitchen door.

"Uh. Jeez, you startled me!"

"Good thing I did. You were letting the cold air out of the fridge! What are you doing?" Charlie asked.

"Deciding. What are you doing? You're home early," I said.

"Came home to pack. Going to New Mexico in the morning. What did you decide?"

"I decided I am hungry. Why are you going to New Mexico?"

"Oh, Toady Mills has passed a hot potato case to us. Bunch of unlicensed graves discovered sliding down a mountainside near Angel Fire. What sounds good? I'm hungry too."

"How about hamburgers and grilled squash?"

"I like it. I'll start the grill," Charlie said as he opened the door to the deck.

"What kind of squash are you thinking?" a familiar

voice said from outside.

Charlie stepped out on the deck and exclaimed, “Burkie!”

I joined Charlie outside and hugged Burkie who was surrounded by a cobalt blue mist. He was wearing, as usual, a black suit and tie, with a white shirt. His thick black hair was combed back as always. His highly polished black shoes reflected the blue light. The wonderful aroma that accompanied Burkie filled the air on the deck.

Immediately, Henry came bounding from the living room, through the kitchen and slid out onto the deck. With a quick bark of greeting, he stood on his back legs to give Burkie a full body big dog hug. Henry is a big dog. As he stood up on his hind legs, his front paws reached Burkie’s shoulders. Burkie hugged him right back. They’ve enjoyed a close friendship for years.

“Henry! You look great old man! How’ve you been?” Burkie said as he helped Henry regain his composure.

Henry sat at Burkie’s feet wagging wildly.

I said, “So nice to see you! Come on in.”

After sitting at the kitchen table chatting for a few minutes, Charlie said, “I’d better start the grill. Can you stay for dinner?”

Burkie replied, “Nothing for me, thanks. But I’ll watch you prepare.”

“Guess you’re here because Charlie is going to New Mexico tomorrow,” I said.

“That is what brought me here today. But I also am always so happy to see you all. How are you?” Burkie replied.

“I’m fine. Tax season has just picked up speed. Henry is doing well. He is a bit older now. I take him to the office with me every day. I think he likes the job element of the routine.

He's my guard."

"Tax work is busy these days," Charlie said. "She has more clients than ever. The multitude of government programs handing out money in different ways in response to the difficulties imposed by those self-same various government agencies in response to the pandemic have created tax concerns for many folks."

I nodded and added, "That's right. So many businesses were blindsided by the lockdown last year, some had to close for good. Others have had to reorganize, reinvent how they do business. Keeping me busy, I can say that."

Burkie said, "Keeps it interesting for you I imagine."

"Yes. It does."

Charlie asked Burkie, "Do you know anything about the New Mexico case I'm about to jump into?"

Burkie smiled and nodded, "I'm able to offer a little information that may prove useful once you get there and begin to understand the situation."

I've known Burkie since I was a toddler. He first appeared when my brother, Ed, and I were very young. Ed and I shared a bedroom. He and I were the closest in age of all the eleven children my parents had. We used to sneak out of our beds at night, sit in our big closet, and peruse picture books. We cleverly stashed books in the closet for these midnight adventures. Often, though, we forgot to put a flashlight in the closet. A flashlight was important because we were too small to reach the pull chain for the ceiling light in the closet. One such night, Ed and I sat on the floor in the dark hatching a plan to go get a flashlight without disturbing anyone in the house. While we were deep in our whispered conference, on the wall in the closet, a thin vertical line of cobalt blue light inexplicably appeared. It grew taller and wider and brighter until it was almost door-size. We were aware of a wonderful aroma accompanying the beautiful light. A tall man, a very handsome smiling man in a black suit and tie with a white shirt stepped out of the blue light. Ed and I were captivated. There was nothing at all frightening about him. He was pure kindness. In the glow of the blue light, we watched the man simply reach for the pull chain and turn on the closet light. He smiled down at us. We thanked him. He stood by until we were ready to steal back to our beds. Our new friend turned the light out for us. Many nights he assisted us with the ceiling light in that closet. In so many ways he has continued to be a caring loving essential part of my life since that very first encounter.

He has been visiting my brother, Ed, and me all of our lives. He just checks in periodically. He has also helped Charlie with various cases by offering counsel and information. He has always looked the same never aged a day in all these years, same clothes, everything the same. And he's always accompanied by that wonderful, comforting smell that I have never encountered anywhere else.

Early in my relationship with Charlie, I told him about Burkie. He listened politely asking few questions. He asked me who or what Burkie was. I explained that Ed and I had asked him that at the beginning. He'd simply replied his name was Burkie. That's all we've ever known. It's been good enough for us all of these decades.

Slowly, eventually, Burkie made himself known to Charlie. It took a while for Charlie to accept Burkie. Now they are close friends. Burkie pops in to help Charlie when he can. I know that Charlie has told his longtime partner FBI Special Agent Jackson Avery about Burkie, and because the help provided has proven useful, both Charlie and Jackson take Burkie seriously. Why wouldn't they? Today sitting at our kitchen table, he looked exactly as he did when I first saw him that night so many years ago.

Charlie asked, "Should I know anything in particular before I get there?"

Burkie replied, "Just that the perpetrator is both clever and careless. The impetus for the murders, and there are multiple murders, seems obscure at this point to me. The energy from these murders is clear and dangerous. The energy betrays a very selfish being. But most murderers are, aren't they?"

"Yes. That's a common denominator!" Charlie said. "Jackson is sending Sam and Carlos, too."

"I'm glad Sam and Carlos are going to join you. Sounds like you will need help," I added.

"All of you need to be alert and use your most highly refined investigative methods. This energy you are looking for is practiced, organized, powerful, and cunning. Though be aware there is somehow energy, maybe some other energy, involved that is sensitive and confused. Opposites swirling in one mass are unstable. As always, please be careful," Burkie said. "And, I will do what I can when I can. As you know, I receive only impressions from energy acting and reacting. But be assured I will also be on alert."

"Yes, I know. And I know a smile can mask all kinds of evil. Thank you. Your input is important to me," Charlie said.

Burkie stood and turned to leave. Henry put his right front paw around Burkie's left calf. Burkie leaned down and hugged Henry's neck.

Burkie told Henry, "Not to worry. I'll be back. Take care of everything here for me."

Henry barked another quick bark and smiled.

The blue glow emerged out of thin air and engulfed

Burkie.

I went to him and gave him a goodbye hug. As I stepped back, Burkie smiled and vanished into the glow, leaving only that wonderful aroma.

"So, that was nice. Burkie will be on the case with me. I like that," Charlie said.

"I like that more than you do," I said.

"I know."

CHAPTER 12

The FBI jet set down at the Taos airport just before noon. The sky was the intense northern New Mexico blue that Charlie always loved to see. The air was crisp and cold. The Santa Fe FBI office had come through with a vehicle. A new black Tahoe was waiting for Charlie at the airport. Standing by the Tahoe were FBI agents Sam Wester and Carlos Sanchez.

"Hey ho, boss!" Sam called out to Charlie. "We beat you here!"

Charlie laughed and said, "Nice to see you. Been waiting long?"

"About an hour or so. We flew into Santa Fe and picked up this SUV from the office there," Carlos explained. "I can tell you it is loaded. It has every gadget and gizmo Chevy has to offer. And it has only seven hundred miles on it!"

"New! That's great. Well let's head to the house. We have a lot of work to do," Charlie said as he tossed his bag in the back. "Carlos, you drive."

Sam took the shotgun seat and Charlie sat in the back.

"We're going to Jackson's rental house?" Carlos asked.

"Yep. It's supposed to be stocked with food and ready for us," Charlie replied.

It was an easy drive from the Taos airport out on the mesa west of town to Jackson's house close to the Taos Plaza.

When they reached the house, they found a state police SUV parked in the driveway. Masked-up Toady Mills stepped out onto the front porch as they parked the Tahoe.

"Hey, FBI people! Hi to you all," Toady called out.

Charlie put on his mask as he got his bag from the rear of the Tahoe. He said to Toady, "Hi. Good to see you!"

Sam and Carlos masked-up and greeted Toady. The men went inside.

Sam asked, "Can I take off the mask inside?"

Toady kept his on, but said, "Strictly speaking it is required in public. Have you been around anyone with Covid?"

Carlos replied, "Well, we just returned from an assignment in Boston, via Chicago, to Santa Fe, and then here. We're vaccinated. Guess we should keep the masks on. I certainly don't want to unknowingly spread anything."

So the men all kept their masks on. Charlie, Sam, and Carlos settled in to their rooms as Toady got a fire going in the fireplace in the big living room.

Charlie emerged from the bedrooms and asked Toady if he was staying for dinner.

Toady replied, "Yes, Andy knows I am on a new case. He never expects me home for anything when I'm in the early stages of an investigation."

"This one has a spooky beginning. Disturbed graves in a heretofore unknown cemetery," Sam said as he joined them in the living room.

Toady, said, "Yes it's a peculiar site, too. Way up in the mountains, and not at all a location anyone would ordinarily come upon. Only poachers, really, would be up there. It's private land surrounded by private land. Not a place legit hunters would be."

Charlie was in the kitchen rummaging through the refrigerator and cabinets. "I know how quickly it gets dark here this time of year. And when it gets dark, I get hungry. So, I'm going to go ahead and fix dinner."

"Great!" Carlos exclaimed. "I just accepted this job for the food. What are we having?"

Charlie said, "We're going to have beef ribeye, and a medley of zucchini, tomatoes, and potatoes. That sound okay to you all?"

Toady replied, "Sounds fabulous to me."

Carlos and Sam agreed. They moved to the dining table in the kitchen area to watch Charlie cook.

Charlie asked Toady, "What can you tell me about the man who owns the property where the cemetery is?"

Toady said, "He's a plumber and a hunting guide named Greg Moranos. He's lived on that property for at about fifteen years I believe. Seems like an interesting guy. He does, or hosts, or whatever the terminology is, a podcast every week."

Sam asked, "Podcast? What about?"

Toady replied, "About his experiences with the supernatural, paranormal, and UAPs and such, and plumbing."

Carlos laughed, "And plumbing?"

"Yeah. Greg's a very well respected plumber. Good plumber. So people ask him plumbing questions all the time."

"What kind of supernatural experiences?" Sam asked. "Your regular ghosts and such?"

"Well maybe. He's encountered energies from other worlds. He's had some sort of interaction with them. He's seen UAPs and shadow beings."

"I look forward to meeting Greg," Charlie said.

Toady said, "We can go there first thing tomorrow if

you want."

Carlos asked Toady, "From the information Jackson provided, Greg Moranos lives on the same property but not near the cemetery site. That accurate?"

"Yes. Greg's house is at the southern end of his land, and the cemetery is located at the northern-most tip. Cemetery's on a peninsula shaped area of his land surrounded on three sides by other property owners' land. All but the house area is forested and sloping. His house sits on a kind of flat shelf area. Nice house. Views are spectacular. Nice deck attached. There's no road from the house to the cemetery. Greg was unaware it was up there," Toady explained.

"How many acres does Greg have?" Carlos asked.

Toady said, "Fifteen or twenty. I'll have to check that."

"It's a pretty big spread," Carlos remarked.

"But it isn't spread out. It's spread up the mountain," Toady added.

Sam said, "So, mountain goats might be our perps. How do you think the bodies were taken to the cemetery?"

Toady responded, "In a pickup truck, through the neighbor's property from a logging road and then on a road forged through the forest onto Greg's land."

"A pickup? How do you know that?" Sam asked.

"Tire tracks. Axel span. Right size for a pickup."

"Oh. Can we get the make and model from those tracks?" Carlos asked.

"I'll bet you can. You're the FBI," Toady said smiling.

Dinner was wonderful. Charlie came through with his customary aplomb in the kitchen. After dinner, the four men sat in the living room enjoying the fire with coffee and cookies. As they discussed the few details known so far about the case, there was a knock at the door.

When Sam opened the door, he saw the large FBI crime scene van. The two agents on the porch stepped inside before Sam could invite them.

"Ooowee it is cold. May we come in," an agent asked after he was standing in front of the fire.

Charlie laughed and said, "Dolph and Marco! Good to see you. Nice drive?"

"Yes. We came down from Denver. It was about a five-hour drive. Went quickly. Marco talked the entire way," Dolph replied.

"You had dinner? We just finished, but I'd be happy to put something together for you," Charlie asked them.

Marco replied, "No. Thanks. We ate on the drive. You know Dolph, he always brings food with him."

Charlie said, "Toady, I'd like you to meet Agents Dolph Menkin and Marco Phenpin. Two of the best CSI agents we have."

Sam exclaimed, "Menkin and Phenpin! Haven't seen you guys in ages. How you been?"

Marco replied, "Just finished a fascinating assignment in Montana. Extreme survivalists had run a preliminary test of their underground facilities. You know, pretending the end had come. But, uh-oh, they inadvertently locked themselves in. No way out. They survived about two weeks. Then they didn't."

Dolph added, "They didn't have enough water in the 'fort,'"

Marco said, "We had to tunnel in so as not to disturb their structure. We had no idea if it was booby-trapped or not. Took a long time to process. They really didn't think it through. It was a poorly designed hideaway."

Toady asked, "Jeez. How many victims?"

"Five large men. They were in a space that might have

accommodated three. They had more ammo and guns than food and water," Marco added.

"Did someone lock them in?" Carlos inquired.

"No. They did it themselves."

"Why'd it take two weeks for anyone to report them missing?" Sam asked.

"I think they told their families that they were going hunting or fishing or something like that. Though I suspect it was just that no one missed them right away," Dolph said.

Marco said, "To be fair, they'd been gone for extended periods before. Guess it took some time to excavate the underground doomsday bunker. Their families might have thought they were working on that. Tom Masters was the lead agent on the case. He can give you all the details. We're just the CSI techs."

Charlie said, "Well I think we have something even more interesting for you two fit young men. A mysterious unexpected cemetery has been discovered up in the mountains over in Colfax County. You'll get to hike and climb and maybe do a little snowshoeing. Sound like fun?"

Marco laughed and said, "You bet it does! When do we start?"

Toady replied, "Tomorrow morning."

CHAPTER 13

It was just before the sun broke the top of the foothills when Toady returned to the house. Everyone was ready to go. With Toady in the lead, the caravan of Toady's police SUV, Charlie, Sam, and Carlos in the FBI Tahoe, and the Dolph and Marco in the FBI CSI van left the Taos house. It took them an hour and a half to reach Greg Moranos' house outside of Angel Fire.

Toady had called ahead and arranged for Greg to be home to meet them. And so Greg stepped out on his porch as the vehicles arrived. Toady Mills introduced everyone in the party: FBI agents Charlie Black, Sam Wester, Carlos Sanchez, Dolph Menkin, and Marco Phenpin.

Greg asked, "Do you think that van can get in to the site?"

Dolph Menkin answered, "It should be able to. It's all-wheel drive. We've tested it many times in some very challenging situations. Always comes through like a champ."

Greg nodded, then he asked Toady if all had been cleared with his neighbor Com Craymist to use his property for access.

"Yes. We're good to go through Com's place. Oh, and he told me he was having Artie survey up there with the intention of fencing his property. He said there've been unauthorized intruders and poaching up there. Have you had any trouble like that?"

Greg replied, "Nope. Not that I'm aware of. If anyone is trespassing on my land, they haven't come by the house here. I have cameras around the house."

Charlie asked him, "Do you check your land? You know, walk or hike it?"

"No, hardly ever. My wife used to hike up the mountain here to bow hunt. But it's been a long time since she did that. She lives down in Angel Fire."

"Are you the only one who lives here?" Charlie asked.

"Yep. Well except for the ghosts and aliens of course," Greg said smiling.

Sam said, "Oh, yeah, I've heard about your podcast. Sounds interesting."

"I have a pretty big following. Seems to be growing every week," Greg explained. "Since you all are going up to the cemetery, any of you want to use a four-wheeler?"

"We're going to drive around and go through Com's place. I don't think we need off-road vehicles....yet. But good to know you have them available if we do need them. Thanks," Toady told him.

"Okay. Call me if you need an assist? I'll be home today," Greg told them.

Again, with Toady in the lead, they left Greg's house and began the long drive-around to Commodore Craymist's land. When they reached the dirt logging road, Toady stopped and walked back to the other vehicles. He asked Charlie if there was any special protocol to follow to help the CSI team.

Charlie asked, "Like what?"

Toady said, "Do they want to go in first?"

"No. Just stop before we reach that area you told me

about, just this side of the cemetery clearing. They should process the tracks found closest to the site."

"Okay. It's slow going from here."

And it was, there had been a little overnight snowfall that left the dirt road even more slippery than Toady remembered it. But, the day promised to be cold and sunny, so they hoped the setup for the scene processing would go as smoothly as possible. When Toady pulled up just short of the entry to the clearing, he turned into the forest as far as he could. Charlie, driving the FBI Tahoe parked next to him. Dolph, driving the van, parked in the road just short of the entry to the clearing. Immediately, the group carefully approached the clearing, walking along the edge of the road and the perceived entry point.

Dolph exclaimed, "Just as described! A hidden cemetery! We need to photograph the area, then we'll set up a couple of enclosed forensic tents. Don't have one tent that'll cover this whole area."

Marco opened the van, which was full of equipment. He launched a small drone to take aerial pictures of the area. Dolph walked the perimeter of the area taking photographs as he went. Then he carefully stepped between the rows of tombstones and graves taking more photos. Toady, Charlie, Sam, and Carlos watched.

Finally, Sam asked, "Hey, Dolph, anything we can do to help?"

Dolph looked up from his digital camera and said, "Yes. Would you please get the white tents from the van? We can set them up as soon as we have a good record of the area as is."

It took another hour before the two enclosed tents were in place over the cemetery area. Marco also set a third enclosed tent in the road just outside of the entry very near the van to serve as a base of operations.

Toady asked Marco as they set up a couple of folding tables in the base tent, "Will these tents hold up to wind and snow?"

"Sure, I'm going to secure them. Have some very long, heavy stakes, and weights to slip into the pockets along the bottoms of the walls. They oughta make it fine," Marco explained.

Charlie stepped into the tent. He asked, "You have a heater, too?"

Marco laughed and said, "Indeed we do. Little solar and battery powered heater. This will be so cozy, you won't want to leave."

Charlie said, "I'm going to invite Emma Spruce to this party. You're going to need some forensic assistance. You okay with that?"

Marco smiled and replied, "Sure, I remember Emma. She still work for New Mexico OMI?"

"Nope. Retired from OMI. She has helped us with a couple of cases since cutting loose from that bureaucratic cluster. I'll give her a call," Charlie said.

Toady suggested they ask Maddy to bring Emma up to the site when she comes. Maddy was planning to join them early afternoon. "She's bringing the 3-D scanner and her file of the scan she made the when she was up here yesterday," Toady said.

At that moment, Maddy's SUV arrived and parked further back down the road. Maddy, Scout, and Emma walked up to the base tent.

"How'd you…?" Charlie began.

Emma laughed and explained, "Jackson called me. He asked me to join the team, so I called your cell. No connection up here I guess. So I called Maddy. She and Scout apprised me of the situation on the drive over. Sounds interesting. How can I help?"

Dolph said, "While Marco is finishing his housekeeping here, let me show you the graves. Can use your help processing this...cemetery."

Sam and Carlos set up and secured the two white enclosed tents over the cemetery per Marco's instructions. The two tents covered the cemetery site. Before the ground disturbances caused by the melting and sliding, the graves had been arranged in three rows of four. The gravity-driven shifting of the tombstones and other evidence had left the area in slight disarray, but the layout was basically the same as the supposed original layout. Each tent covered six now somewhat sloppy graves, three rows of two.

As Marco carefully arranged his equipment on the tables in the base tent, he said to Maddy Lucero, "Toady says you took a 3-D scan of the area. Did you bring it?"

Maddy took a flash drive from her uniform pocket and handed it to Marco. She said, "I have only seen it once, and that was quickly."

Toady added, "Me, too."

Marco queued up the scan file on his laptop. As they watched the scan, they saw the same thing at the same time.

Toady gasped, "Jeez. I didn't notice that when I saw this before!"

Maddy said, "Me either!"

Charlie said, "I didn't see it either. Is that what I think it is?"

Marco Phenpin said, "I believe it is."

The scan was in sharp detail on the laptop screen. Beyond the graves, in the trees beyond, they saw a figure, a shadowy figure wearing a western style hat looking out from behind a tree. The 3-D camera caught it swaying as it watched what they were doing.

"Who was here that day?" Charlie asked.

Toady answered, "Me, Maddy, and Sheriff's Deputy Marvin McShine. Marvin and I stood to the side as Maddy made this 3-D recording. I'll admit my focus was on the graves. But how did we all miss that, whatever it is, watching us?"

They continued watching the recording. As Maddy changed the direction of the 3-D camera, the camera kept recording. She slowly panned away from where the figure was visible in the trees and then back, the figure had disappeared.

Charlie said to Maddy, "Bring Scout. Let's go check that spot where the shadow cowboy was."

"Shadow cowboy? Who's that?" Sam asked as he and Carlos entered the base tent.

Marco said, "You have to see this."

He played the recording again.

Sam and Carlos both exclaimed, "Cool. Ghosts!"

Charlie said, "We'll see if Scout can pick up a ghost scent. Come on Maddy."

When Scout got to the tree they determined the shadowy figure had been standing behind, he did find a scent to track. Maddy instructed him to follow and find. Scout slowly circled around through the trees, and then went straight to the cemetery to a tent, the tent that'd been labeled #1. He went in the tent and sat by a grave. It was the grave with the discarded corn chip bag and mud-encrusted cell phone next to it.

Dolph and Emma entered the tent. Scout didn't move a muscle. Maddy said, "Good boy, Scout. Stand down."

Scout relaxed and sat by Maddy.

"What's happening?" Dolph asked. "Why are you guys

tramping through my crime scene?"

"Ghost hunting," Charlie replied. He explained what they'd seen on the 3-D recording and what Scout had discovered.

Emma said, "Interesting. A cowboy ghost."

"Or something," Charlie added.

CHAPTER 14

The FBI forensic technicians, Dolph Menkin and Marco Phenpin were ready to begin their meticulous processing of the scene. In full body Tyvek suits, Dolph assisted by Emma Spruce began in tent #1, and Marco assisted by Toady Mills, also in Tyvek suits, worked in tent #2. They treated the cemetery much as an anthropological dig site. They marked off each grave with wooden stakes and string. Each partition would be carefully excavated and catalogued.

Maddy and Scout led the way through the surrounding forest. Charlie, Sam, and Carlos followed behind without contaminating any area before Scout could cover it. They carefully photographed and investigated every tree and as much of the snowy, muddy ground as possible.

As each of the teams in the tents found artifacts or body parts, the evidence was tagged and bagged and delivered to the base tent. The space in the base tent quickly filled. Depositing the most recently filled body bag in the base tent, Emma and Dolph had no option but to slide it under a table.

Dolph said, "We'd better get the transport van up here to take these bodies and their parts to Albuquerque. Need to have autopsies ASAP."

Emma asked, "FBI transport?"

"Yes. We asked for one this morning. Hope it's at least

made it as far as Santa Fe by now. I'll check with Charlie," Dolph said.

Dolph found Charlie deep in the woods with Maddy and Scout. "Any word on the transport van?" Dolph asked.

Charlie looked up and said, "Oh. I'll try to call now. Have to use my satellite phone. The cell service up here is thin to nothing. The phone's in the Tahoe."

Charlie and Dolph headed for the Tahoe parked in the trees a distance before the entry road. On the way, Dolph saw something at the base of a big pine tree.

"What's this?" Dolph said.

He stooped and retrieved a small piece of something. Charlie turned back and looked at what Dolph was holding.

"What is it?" Charlie asked.

"It's the business end of an arrow. This is a fixed broadhead, the point. Not an ancient one. A very modern one. This is from an arrow used in a compound or cross bow. The nock might have had a small led light on it. It helps the hunter see where the game is hit. And it helps the hunter find his arrow if it goes all the way through or misses."

"So, where's the arrow?"

Dolph said, "Might be close by."

The two men carefully searched the area. No arrow. Dolph bagged and tagged the broadhead. They continued on to the Tahoe and Charlie called the Albuquerque FBI lab. The transport van was on its way. They were told it should arrive at the site within the hour.

As they walked back to the base tent, Charlie asked, "Any cause of death obvious on anything you've recovered so far?"

"Yes. Emma found a male with a broken arrow shaft still lodged through the torso. Came in from the back and seems to have gone right through the heart. The tip of the broadhead is just sticking out of the clothes on the chest."

"Shot in the back. That's cold. Anything else you noticed?" Charlie asked.

"We've found two tombstones with no bodies buried, but the other four in our tent are occupied graves," Dolph said. "Nothing is buried deep. In fact they are barely buried. And the dirt under the bodies is undisturbed. So we don't think there are any double decker graves. The excavations are going quickly. Some bodies are garbed in only underwear, some have only pants and shirts. No shoes so far."

Charlie stopped walking, he said, "That's odd, don't you think?"

Dolph said, "Yes, very."

"Let's check with Marco and Toady," Charlie said as he hurried on.

When they reached tent #2, Marco and Toady were kneeling on tarps on the ground focused on two different graves.

Charlie said, "Hi. So what've you found so far?"

Marco looked up and replied, "Some unexpected things, though I don't know what I expected. For instance, we seem to have three tombstones here that mark nothing. In the found graves, the victims are all male. Not all the bodies are intact. A couple of graves have been robbed by animals. Some are dressed, but with only underwear, or pants and a t-shirt. No shoes, no watches, no rings. From the two tents, we've found a cell phone, a bag of corn chips, part of a pizza box, no pizza, a coke can, and a fitbit."

"Are the bodies in similar states of decomp?" Charlie asked.

"Not at all. Some are far gone, and there is one that is

fairly fresh."

Dolph added, "Same in tent #1, some are lots older than others."

Charlie said, "I look forward to seeing your mapping of the cemetery with those graves that held bodies and those with no bodies and artifacts marked along with apparent stages of decomp. I'm hoping there is some kind of pattern to the layout. The transport van should be here any time now. We can get the body bags to the FBI's ABQ lab for autopsy ASAP."

Charlie and Dolph went to tent #1. Emma was sitting on a small tarp on the ground next to a grave. She was busy entering data into a tablet. She looked up when they entered the tent.

"Oh there you are, Dolph," she said. "I just found something interesting."

Emma held up a large oval shaped ornately decorated western belt buckle. She handed it to Dolph. He put on a fresh pair of latex gloves to receive the buckle. He turned it around and examined it carefully. Charlie looked over his shoulder.

"Ah ha, an inscription. Good," Charlie said.

"It says, 'In God We Trust' and then has a date of June 30, 1999," Dolph reported. "What does that mean?"

Charlie shrugged. "Hope Jackson can figure that out."

Emma said, "It was under the right leg of this body. Under the calf."

Charlie said, "That's the grave Scout led us to as he tracked from the shadow cowboy's location in the trees."

Emma said, "Interesting. Maybe this is that cowboy's buckle."

Charlie left Dolph with Emma in tent #1. He returned to the base tent. Maddy, Scout, Sam, and Carlos were all seated in the tent talking and drinking hot coffee.

"What's up?" Sam asked Charlie.

"Transport's on the way. Tents #1 and #2 are finding some unoccupied graves, and some artifacts with the bodies or near the bodies. Some bodies are older than others," Charlie reported. "An arrow killed one victim. And Dolph found a lone fixed broadhead, at the base of a tree near the entry to site. We looked for the arrow shaft, but no luck."

"Bet there are hundreds of bow hunters in this county," Maddy said.

"That's gotta be true," Carlos agreed.

"Do poachers favor bows over guns?" Charlie asked Maddy.

She replied, "No. Not really. If they are hunting, poaching, near any populated area, they might use bows just for stealth's sake."

Carlos said, "The bow hunters, that I know, are passionate about the sport of bow hunting."

Sam said, "What? What bow hunters do you even know?"

"Some. Online."

"What. You have bow-hunter friends online? I don't buy it," Sam remarked.

"I do."

"You do not."

Charlie said, "How about you all work that out later. Right now I'd like you to do a little FBI investigative research into bow hunting. Get the broadhead from Dolph. He bagged it. And find out, if possible, what make and model of arrow or kind of bow it might have been used with. All I know is that crossbows and compound bows use similar but different arrows and broadheads. Crossbows can also use projectiles call bolts. Those are not arrows. We'll have to see what the forensics tells us about what exactly was used with which victim."

Maddy said, "Scout found a clear scent trail that encircles the cemetery. It is about thirty feet back in the woods from the clearing. It seems to be well trod. He had no issue finding it and staying on it."

Sam said, "I wonder if the trodder of the trail is the perp just doing due diligence reconnoitering with each burial. You know, just to make sure nobody's intruding on the trespass."

Charlie laughed, "Could be. The shadow cowboy was at about that distance from the cemetery."

"When will we get the make and model of the tires and hopefully the vehicle that made the entry tracks?" Maddy asked.

Charlie said, "I'll upload all the new info to Jackson tonight. Should have results by morning."

"I can get an APB out as soon as you let me know," Maddy told him.

Carlos said to Maddy, "I hope it's not a Ford F150. There are jillions of those."

Charlie said, "Jackson'll narrow it down as much as possible. He's going to get a lot of data from us tonight. Hope by tomorrow, we can begin to move this evidence collection phase into the catch the perp phase. Oh, think I hear the transport van."

The FBI transport van backed up to the entry point. The agents said a quick hello to everyone and then began putting body bags into the van.

"Jackson gave us strict instructions to get this load to the lab as fast as possible. Are there any more bags?" an agent asked Charlie.

"Let's check," he replied.

The two agents followed Charlie to tent #1. Dolph

and Emma had two more bags ready to go. They said that was it for them. Tent #2 had one more bag and that was all they thought they'd have. All found graves were cleaned out. The agents loaded the last bags into the van. They headed for Albuquerque.

Charlie said to Toady and Marco in tent #2, "It getting late. I think we should make some decisions. Do you think we should work through the night? Or should we secure the site and come back in the morning?"

Marco said, "We have lights. Dolph and I'll keep going."

Charlie said, "It is going to be very very cold, zero or below. Might be better to return in the morning. This is so remote that it's unlikely to be bothered by anyone overnight. Well, except the perp."

"Dolph and I have to stay with the scene. We usually camp in the base tent or the van when we're on a job. We have a heater, and food. We'll be fine. We'll keep an eye on everything," Marco explained.

"Okay. I'll let everyone know. Do you have a satellite phone?" Charlie said.

"We do."

"Okay. And if shadow cowboy shows up, please interview him and get pictures," Charlie added.

When Charlie returned to the base tent, Sam asked him, "Want me to pack up these artifacts to send to the Dallas forensics lab?"

"That was going to be my next request. When we get back to Taos, you can take them to the airport. An FBI plane is there and waiting to whisk them to Dallas. The artifacts and the autopsies are our path to identifying these victims, and, I hope, the perp," Charlie said.

Carlos added, "Unless shadow cowboy can tell us who they are, who did this, and why the hell they were buried here."

CHAPTER 15

The following morning, Toady called Charlie at the house. "You want to sit in on Greg's podcast production session? He's invited you and any of your team to come to his house today at noon."

Charlie replied, "Yes I do. I'll bring whoever wants to join us. Are you going to be there?"

"Yes. And Maddy is coming with me. You know, the horse stall black shadow story" Toady said.

After the call, Charlie immediately asked his investigators if anyone wanted to witness Greg's podcast.

Sam responded, "You bet I do!"

Carlos had similar enthusiasm for the opportunity. He asked Charlie, "What do you hear from the cemetery this morning? Dolph and Marco made it through the night?"

"Yes. They had a cold night they said even with a heater. But all was quiet. They're continuing with the excavation of the areas around the graves. Next they'll expand their efforts to the area around the cemetery site."

Sam noted, "They really love what they do. They love scratching in the dirt."

Carlos laughed, "Yes the FBI offers all sorts of career opportunities for all sorts of people."

At noon, the FBI agents met up with Toady and Maddy

at Greg Moranos' house. As they were climbing the steps to his front porch, a Subaru bounded up the driveway. Emma Spruce jumped out.

Toady said, "Glad you could make it."

Emma replied, "Glad you invited me."

Greg opened the door, "Wow, a pod of podcast fans! Come in."

Inside, Greg led them to a room off the fireplace end of the great room. It had been a bedroom, but was now converted to a rather sophisticated broadcast studio. One wall was filled with shelves of computer and sound equipment. Another wall was covered with sound baffling foam panels. Greg had set up folding chairs around a central table. Everyone found a seat.

Charlie said, "I didn't expect such an extensive array of equipment. Do all podcasters have setups like this?"

"Oh no. I just kinda like the tech side of this. I like to upgrade whenever something new is available. I only use a fraction of what you see here for the podcast. It's a simple procedure in a complex-looking setting," Greg replied laughing at himself.

Sam said, "So, Greg, tell me what you are doing today?"

Greg responded, "Good question to begin an interview. Today I am recording my podcast. After recording, I will edit it and then upload it to my host manager. Then my hosting service will published it and make it available for listening. My show's broadcast schedule is maintained by the hosting service. When I post to them, they will notify my known listeners that the episode will be available at a certain time. My show is usually broadcast on Tuesday evening at nine. The hosting service has a directory online, so you can find what you want to listen to."

Carlos asked, "So you record and edit your show here?"

Greg answered, "Exactly. The software I use allows me to edit and hone my shows before I upload. Kinda foolproof."

Toady asked, "Do you interview guests here?"

"Yes, I have. But I can also interview remotely via apps like Skype, or Zoom, or Squadcast. I like Squadcast. It is easy to use and the audio is very good. The interview can be recorded, then I edit and fit it into my show as I feel it will best work."

"Interesting. Do you make money with a podcast?" Emma asked.

"You can. I don't. Some people use advertising, marketing, subscriptions."

"Why do you do it?' she pressed.

"Because I enjoy sharing my experiences, and I enjoy hearing others' experiences. I've learned so much from my listeners."

Charlie asked, "How do your listeners interact with you if it's not live?"

"Email. I get emails every day. I respond to them on the show. If someone emails me while I'm recording, I may insert that interaction into that show," Greg explained.

Sam asked, "How do you describe the content of your podcast? Keywords?"

Greg laughed and replied, "It's a movable feast, evolving, so to speak. I usually just talk about my most recent experience of a paranormal sort, or sightings and interactions with unidentified phenomenon. I also answer questions about plumbing problems. I am a plumber after all."

"Are you going to interview us?" Toady asked.

"I'd like to ask Maddy to tell her story of the dark mass in the horse barn. That was a compelling testament. As a law enforcement officer, she is a legitimate witness," Greg said, looking at Maddy.

Maddy responded, "Sure. I'd be happy to recount that experience."

"Okay. Great. Let me get a few things ready here. While recording, I'll set this two-sided mike here on the table. If you would talk in a normal tone and volume it will be able to pick up fine."

Charlie remarked, "Your mike looks like an old-time radio show mike."

Greg smiled, "Yes, it does. I've found it's a mike that works very well for recording without having to have it right in front of your mouth. Good for in-person interviews."

Greg quickly was ready to begin. He gave his usual intro into the show, thanking his listeners for their time and responses. He then read a few emails and responded. The masked group assembled remained quiet and attentive.

Greg then told his listeners that he had some guests in the studio. He said, "Today I am honored to have with me a number of law enforcement officers. One of which is going to recount an experience she had while investigating a case. Maddy? Would you introduce yourself?"

Maddy introduced herself to the invisible audience and told the story of the manifestation of the dark mass in the horse stall. She didn't give any details of the case that took her to the barn, nor where it was. Greg didn't press her for any details, as he understood that she was appropriately presenting the experience for the audience.

When Maddy finished her story, Greg asked the group at the table if anyone else had any supernatural experiences to relate. Charlie raised his hand.

Greg said, "Okay. We have another contribution, from

an FBI agent."

Charlie introduced himself and began, "I have witnessed many extraordinary events while investigating crimes involving the worst of human behavior, murder. I have seen what I can only describe as released human spirit energy, usually in the form of brightly colored light, balls of light, or streams of light. The victims' life energy manifesting near the site of death. Sometimes the lights assist in the resolution of the crime. Sometimes it appears the lights are on their way to the next dimension or somewhere. It is always incredible and beautiful to watch."

Greg said, "My lord! I wasn't expecting that from you, Charlie. Wow."

Emma interrupted, introduced herself, and said "In my many years of working for the Office of the Medical Investigator, I investigated unattended deaths and suspicious deaths. The visible spirit energy Charlie described is not at all uncommon. The lights are truly beautiful and seem comforting in a way."

Greg asked her, "Do these spirit energies communicate with you?"

Charlie answered, "I have knowledge of voice communication from murder victims at or near the scene of death. But the lights don't talk, though they can appear to be interacting with each other when there are clusters of them."

Greg said, "Goodness. I had no idea. Do you think the victims are trying to help you solve their murders?"

"Simply stated, yes," Charlie replied.

Sam said, "I've witness light phenomenon that definitely was making an effort to help us with murder investigations."

Greg asked him to introduce himself and elaborate.

Sam introduced himself and then continued, "I personally have seen a bright green light that behaved like a liquid. It flowed under a closed door and across the floor. It was letting us know where to look. I've seen that same green liquid light in different situations on different investigations. It has always been a direct help in our investigations. "

Carlos added, "I've witnessed that, too."

Greg asked, "Have you seen such lights on your current investigation?"

Charlie answered, "No, not yet. But we have caught a shadow figure manifestation on a recording near the scene."

Greg looked shocked. He asked, "Was the shadow figure a help to you?"

"Remains to be seen," Charlie said.

Sam and Carlos laughed. Sam said, "Remains at the scene! Pun!"

Greg said, "Good to see you all can maintain levity in your line of work."

Carlos said, "Have to, in order to maintain sanity."

"Greg, what recent encounters have you had here?" Charlie asked.

Greg said, "My listeners will recall my ongoing visits by a black shape. I had another visit not long ago. At night, on my back deck, it seemed to be watching the house. I can feel when it is here. I don't always see it, but this time I did. It was a full moon and the snow was bright. The black shape did not communicate. It is always unnerving, but this time it was more frightening than usual. Since it took my energy out of my physical self on a previous visit, I have learned to control my thoughts, not to ask it anything. I don't want it to answer me. I am scared of it."

Emma said, "Interesting. Is it always outside? Never been seen inside the house?"

Greg replied, "Always outside."

Charlie asked, “Have you ever recorded its visit?”

“No. It doesn’t trip the outside security cameras. It stays just beyond the coverage zone. I am going to set up other cameras out past the deck. I do plan to capture it on camera,” Greg explained.

The recording session lasted about an hour. Greg gave his usual outro spiel and concluded the recording. He thanked everyone and the group dispersed.

As they were getting into their respective vehicles, Charlie invited them to come to the house. He suggested it was time for a quick debriefing.

CHAPTER 16

"So what is your take on Greg Moranos?" Charlie began once they were all seated in the living room.

"How does he have so much computer equipment in his studio, and some outside security cameras, and yet has not put enough cameras outside to capture the scary night visitor?" Sam asked.

Carlos said, "Yeah. That seems odd. He's obviously a serious techy."

Toady said, "He is a strange guy. I can't decide if I think he's capable of murder. He certainly could have created the cemetery, but murder?"

Charlie said, "He really could be our perp. But we have a lot to determine before we go there."

"What do we know from Jackson?" Sam asked.

"He got the artifacts very early this morning. Everything is at the lab. The autopsies are underway in ABQ. Denver FBI sent additional forensics techs to Albuquerque to assist our people there and expedite the autopsies. Hopefully we'll begin to get IDs on the victims maybe as soon as later today. I've been thinking about a profile of the perp. It's a puzzle as yet… with no picture to go by. We need more info, of course. I think we should interview Greg's wife as well as people who know them," Charlie said.

Toady said, "James Frustini and his wife, Susan Mileser have a construction company in Angel fire. Greg is one of their subs. And Susan is friends with Kako Williams, Greg's wife."

Sam said, "Kako? Not heard that name before. Short for something?"

Emma Spruce answered, "It's short for Kakoahulani. Her mother was Hawaiian."

Carlos asked, "You know her?"

"No. But I've been in her store. She has an antique store in Angel Fire. I asked her," Emma replied.

"Oh. What kind of antiques?" Carlos asked.

"All kinds, some furniture, some fixtures, some clothes, some other equipment and stuff. Not all of it is actually antique. But most all of it is older or used," Emma explained. "Since the Covid, she's taken the store online."

"Let's look at her online store. What's it called?" Charlie said.

Emma replied, "I think it is the same as her real store, 'For All Time.'"

Charlie got the store's site on his laptop screen. They all crowded around him to look.

Carlos said, "She sells everything. She even has camping and hunting equipment."

Maddy said, "Well, remember, Greg is a hunting guide."

"That's right, he is. So why doesn't he include hunting as a podcast topic?" Sam asked.

"Good question for an interview," Carlos quipped.

"Maddy, can you setup an interview with Frustini and Mileser? Maybe for this afternoon?" Charlie asked.

"I'll call right now."

Charlie said, "Sam, you and Carlos talk to them. Ask

them any and everything you can think of."

Toady said, "Maddy and I can interview Kako Williams."

"Great, thanks. Emma, can you go back to the cemetery with me?" Charlie asked.

Emma said, "Yes. Now?"

"As soon as I fix some food for Dolph and Marco. I don't think they were prepared for this long of a stint at the site. Oh, and can we go in your car? Sam and Carlos will have the Tahoe."

Sam asked, "Can we have food, too?"

Charlie laughed and said, "Yes. Give me a minute to make a late lunch for us all. After we eat, we can scatter and solve this case!"

CHAPTER 17

Sam and Carlos had no trouble finding Frustini's construction company office in Angle Fire. As Maddy had arranged, James and Susan were there waiting for them. Once introductions were made, the masked foursome sat near the woodstove in the office for the meeting.

"So, Maddy Lucero said you wanted to ask us some questions. You working on that cemetery Artie found up at Greg's place? You find bodies buried there?" James asked Sam.

"Exactly. Yes we have removed a number of bodies from the site. We're hoping you can tell us about the people who own the land, about Greg and his wife."

Susan said, "We've known them for many years. They're nice people."

"I've met Greg. He does seem like a nice guy," Carlos noted.

"Greg is a super plumber. The best around here," James Frustini told them.

Sam asked, "Kako Williams has a retail store, 'For All Time.' How long has she had the store?"

Susan Mileser answered, "Oh, I think at least five or six years. It did pretty well until the pandemic. The lockdown hit all the retailers hard. But Kako put it online and she's been doing well with that. She is smart and a good salesperson. And she's usually got a wide variety of inventory. It's an antique store, but it has other stuff, too. She sells used stuff, too."

"I was told you are friends with her. How long have you known her?" Sam asked.

"Seems like I've known her since she and Greg moved here about maybe fifteen or so years ago."

"Where did they come from?"

"James, do you remember where they lived before?" Susan asked her husband.

James thought for a second, then said, "I think they moved here from California. At first, they rented a condo from us. Then about fifteen years ago they bought the land where Greg lives now. We built that house."

Carlos said, "It's a nice house. We sat in on a podcast recording session today. Greg is really into his podcast."

James laughed, "He sure is. He's a busy guy. You know he's a hunting guide as well as a plumber."

Carlos asked, "Hunting seasons keep him busy throughout the fall and winter?"

"The hunting is all up at a huge ranch. Since they are private land hunts, Greg can sell as many hunts as he can buy tags for. They have lion, elk, deer, bighorns, bears, and a few exotic deer and antelope. It's a beautiful ranch," James explained.

"So when he's guiding, he lives at the ranch? The hunts are more than a day long aren't they? Where do his hunters stay?" Sam asked.

"I'm not sure if his schedule is always the same for every hunt, most hunts are few days at least. He did tell me the hunters stay at the big house at the ranch. The ranch belongs to the Flowerdale heirs, you know the cosmetic company

Flowerdales. The senior Flowerdales lived at the ranch. Very nice large house. The seniors have been dead for quite a few years now. The heirs don't live here. I don't think they even come out here anymore. Greg leases the house and the whole ranch for his guide business," James told them.

"Is that a lucrative business?" Carlos asked.

James laughed and replied, "Yes, it is very lucrative. Hunting guides do well. Some better than others. Greg does very well. No one else hunts that ranch. It is ideal. His customers come from all over the country. And they pay big bucks for hunts."

"Bucks! I get it! Good one. Guess these are trophy hunters then?" Sam asked.

"I think most are. If they drive here, they can take the meat home. But if they fly or just don't want the meat, the local guides give the meat to the food banks. That's what most all the guides do. It's a lot of meat. And the hunters have to pay for the processing whether they take the meat or not. Once the head or hide is mounted, it can be shipped to them. That's no small ticket item."

"How much does a hunt cost?" Carlos asked.

James said, "I'm guessing, but I'd imagine it's in the range of at least ten to fifteen grand for a few days' hunt for elk, for instance."

"Jeez. That's more than I'd have guessed," Sam said. "So only rich people go on these hunts?"

James said, "Absolutely. They have travel expenses, too. It's not a sport for everyone. Kind of like skiing. It takes no small amount of disposable cash to enjoy certain pastimes."

"Guess so!" Carlos said.

Sam asked, "I understand that Kako is a hunter. Is that true?"

"Yes she is. She used to hunt a lot. But as her store has taken more and more time, she has less time to do other things, like hunt. She does join Greg and his hunters now and then," Susan explained.

Carlos asked, "I know Kako doesn't live with Greg. Where does she live?"

Susan answered, "She rents a home over by the country club lake, here in Angel Fire."

"Why doesn't she live up at their house? It's a nice house. It looks big."

Susan continued, "She told me she just can't live with Greg. He is so…intense about things. She feels more comfortable living here in town."

"He seems like a smart guy. He wasn't strange acting or anything today as he recorded his podcast. He does talk, very casually in fact, about his paranormal encounters. He really doesn't come off as a nutter like some of the people I've dealt with who interact with the unknown dimensions," Sam noted.

James said, "That's right. That's how he is with me. Seems perfectly normal to talk about aliens, ghosts, and stuff like that. He's a regular guy. It's just the topics are different from most."

The construction office door opened to admit a tall late middle-aged man wearing a fur hat and a large coat, along with a blast of cold air.

"Hop! Come in," James said.

James introduced Hop Sovern to the FBI agents.

Hop said, "Sorry to intrude. Everything okay?"

Sam said, "We're just asking questions. We're investigating the newly found cemetery on Greg Moranos' land. Are you familiar with that?"

As he took off his coat and hat, donned his mask, and

joined them by the woodstove, Hop answered, "I've heard about it. Everyone in the county has heard about what Artie found up there. It's all anyone talks about. What have you found out?"

Sam said, "Still early in the investigation. Right now we're gathering info. Do you have any notion as to who might be responsible for the cemetery there?"

"Nope. Who's buried there?" Hop asked.

"Don't have IDs yet," Carlos said.

Hop said, "When you do, maybe their families will be able to help you."

Susan said, "Good idea. Maybe it is a family cemetery. Maybe the family is using it."

Carlos explained, "There is no cemetery at that location shown on any maps, new or old. Nor is there any registration of a cemetery at that location. Greg says he's sure it wasn't there when he bought the property years ago. There was evidence at the site of recent activity. You are right about the IDs of the dead being important. That should give us a leg-up on the case."

Sam laughed, "Leg-up! Body part! Good one."

Carlos asked, "Do you all listen to Greg's podcasts?"

Hop said, "I've heard a few. He's good at it. Keeps the topics interesting and relatable, even when the subject matter is way off in left field."

Sam said, "Yes. We saw him in action firsthand today. We sat in on a recording session."

James said, "Many people around this area see UAPs. In fact, we see them pretty often. It's not a big deal anymore. Greg has had interaction with things that most people don't. That's interesting to hear about. He's a very smart guy who lives a little on the edge. He's experienced the edge. He talks about it just like he talks about putting in a new plumbing system."

Carlos asked Hop, "Do you know Greg's wife, Kako?"

Hop answered, "Yes. She's a very beautiful and very smart woman. She has a little store here in town."

"You shop at her store?" Carlos asked.

"Stop in there every so often. Always nice to see her. I've bought some gear from her. Good prices."

"What do you mean, gear?"

Hop replied, "Oh, hunting stuff. Got a rifle scope, a nice winter camo jacket, got some ammo, boots. Got my fur hat from her."

He motioned towards the coat rack where he'd hung the hat.

Sam got up and asked, "May I look at the hat?"

"Sure," Hop replied.

"This is a nice hat! It's like new. What kind of fur is this?" Sam asked him.

"Coon. Just like Davy and Daniel!" Hop said laughing. "Just no tail!"

"Bet it's warm."

"You bet right," Hop said. "Best winter hat I've ever had."

Carlos said, "From what I'm hearing, Kako sells a bit of everything."

Susan said, "Yeah. She does. Always has a lot to look at."

"You're not looking at Greg and Kako as the cemetery killers, are you?" James asked.

Carlos answered, "We're looking everywhere at this point. And they are the owners of the site."

"Seems crazy for someone to bury their victims on their own property," Susan remarked.

"It happens all the time. People kill and then bury the

bodies in their own back yard or under their own house. It isn't easy to dispose of a human body. If this is a serial killer, then they sometimes find a dump site or sites that they can use over and over," Carlos explained.

Sam added, "Right now, we have to establish who the dead are and causes of death."

"When will you know that?" Susan asked.

"Soon. The bodies are being autopsied as we speak."

CHAPTER 18

When New Mexico State Police Criminal Investigator Toady Mills and Officer Maddy Lucero arrived outside of Kako Williams' store, "For All Time," it was dark inside and closed.

Maddy said, "I spoke to her about a half hour ago. She said she'd be here. Let's give her a few more minutes. If she doesn't show, I'll call again."

"Okay. Maybe this is her now," Toady said pointing at a black Ford F150 that was just turning into the parking lot.

A tall, attractive, dark-haired woman wearing a long fur-trimmed winter coat, jeans, and snow boots, stepped out of the Ford pickup. She smiled and waved at the state police officers. Toady and Maddy met her at the door of the store.

Putting her mask on as she unlocked the door, Kako greeted them with, "Hello. Hope I haven't kept you waiting!"

After all introductions were made, the masked-up officers followed her into the store and stood by the door until she'd turned on the lights. She invited them to sit in the homey arrangement of chairs near her checkout counter. When she took off her coat and laid it across the counter, they could see how long her hair was. Her dark straight shiny hair reached halfway down her back.

Maddy said, "Love your hair!"

Kako, removed her mask, smiled, and replied, "Oh

Thanks! Inherited from my mother. She was a native Hawaiian. So, what can I help you with today?"

Toady kept his mask on and said, "We're investigating the discovery of bodies in an unregistered cemetery on your land."

"My land? Where?" Kako said.

"The property that you and your husband, Greg Moranos, own, and where he lives," Maddy clarified. "Your name is on the deed as well as his."

"Do you have other land?" Toady asked.

"No. No. I don't. I just think of that place up there as his."

"Do you know about the discovery of the graves up there?" Maddy asked.

"I have heard some talk about a cemetery that Artie Tibbets found. But I didn't know it was on our land," Kako said.

"Greg didn't tell you?" Toady posed.

"I don't remember. He tells me so many outrageous things. I hardly listen to him anymore," Kako replied smiling.

"What kind of outrageous things?" Maddy asked.

Kako laughed and said, "Oh, if you knew Greg! He lives in a world all his own. He visits with aliens, paranormal beings. He sees things. He's mentally ill, I'm afraid."

Toady said, "We sat-in with him during a podcast recording session today. He was charming, cogent, and seemed fine."

Kako's face went blank for a second, then she recovered, smiled, and said, "He can appear as fine as you and me. He does manage to hold a couple of jobs. He's a plumber and a hunting guide. He has his podcast hobby. But he also time-travels and has a complicated imaginary life."

Toady said, "You don't live with him. Why not? That's a lovely house."

"It is easier and more comfortable for us both for us to live apart. I visit him often. I make or take dinner up there when I can."

"You always go where he lives? Does he ever visit you?"

"I live in a rental over near the lake. He doesn't come into town often. I go up to his house. It is a very nice house. He likes it up there. Has his studio there. So I live down here close to town."

From behind her mask, Maddy smiled at her and said, "And you have your store here. This is nice. Goodness you have a lot of merchandise."

The unmasked Kako smiled and said, "Oh yes. You should look around. You'll find all kinds of treasures."

"We'd love to," Toady said.

The masked state police officers began a slow shopping stroll through the sizable store. Toady found a camo winter coat and winter boots.

He asked Kako, "Are these new? They look new."

Kako replied, "Nearly new. I don't think they've ever been used."

"Great deal. I'd like to try them on."

Kako smiled and asked him to follow her. She led him to the back of the store to a short hallway with louvered doors on each side.

"Here you go. You can use the changing room here," Kako said as she opened the door on the right side of the hallway.

While Toady was trying the clothes, Maddy was perusing some sports equipment.

"Finding anything you love?" Kako asked her.

"You've got skis, snowshoes, hiking poles, tennis rackets, all kinds of outdoor boots, and coats. I was told you have an antique store," Maddy stated in a questioning tone.

Kako smiled and said, "I started out as an antique store. But branched out as my customers requested other items. It's been a learning and growing experience."

"I guess so. You still have some nice antique furniture and lamps. They make good display pieces, don't they?"

"Yes. My customers are not too interested in antique furniture these days. They're more practically minded. This pandemic has changed everything. I do have an online store. I feature everything you see here. And because nearly everything is a one-of-a-kind, it's takes constant upkeep of my site to put merchandise pics up and take them down as items come in and then sell."

"How long have you been here?" Maddy asked.

"Greg and I moved here from southern California eighteen years ago. We'd never been here before that. We read about Angel Fire in a real estate magazine. It looked beautiful. And, we were ready to get away from the congestion. I opened this store six years ago."

"Were you in retail in California?"

"No. We both worked for a dot-com business that failed. It was time for something new. Those were different days!" Kako said.

"That's true! Where do you get your merchandise?" Maddy asked.

"Various sources. Some of this is here on consignment." She waved her hand at her displays. "Some of it I get from estate sales in Santa Fe or Taos. Or I buy it online myself if a customer asks for something in particular." Kako explained.

Toady returned from the changing room and said, "I'll take these." He handed the coat and boots to Kako.

"Splendid! Need gloves?" Kako said as she moved around behind the checkout counter. "I have a good selection of winter gloves for men. Look in that cabinet." She pointed to a china cabinet with doors open and a display of gloves and scarves on the shelves.

Toady looked at the gloves, picked a pair of nylon and knit gloves. "These look like winter shooting gloves," he said to Kako.

"I think you're right. Do they fit?" Kako responded.

"They fit like a glove! I'll take 'em," Toady replied with a laugh and smile.

Maddy asked Kako, "I know Greg guides. Do you ever go on hunts with him?"

Kako smiled and said, "I have enjoyed hunting for years. I do join Greg's hunting groups sometimes. I just don't have much time to do that."

"I hear the house at the Timberlake Ranch is very nice. Do you stay there?" Maddy asked.

"Oh that house is quite a showplace. The Flowerdales always did everything first-class. It was featured in several national magazines way back when it was first built. The house is part of the draw for Greg's clientele. They look forward to seeing the house as much as hunting! To stay in the house is such a treat for them. It's been updated and remodeled through the years, but it's held its original charm and good looks," Kako said.

"Just like me!" Toady remarked laughing.

Kako smiled and wrapped his purchases. Toady handed her a credit card. She took it and slipped the chip end into her machine. She handed it back to Toady who carefully slipped it into his shirt pocket. He and Maddy thanked Kako for meeting with them.

"If there is anything else that you think I can help you with, just call. Thank you for your business!" Kako said as she let them out the door.

She relocked the door as they walked away.

CHAPTER 19

Emma drove Charlie to the cemetery. They brought a cardboard banker's box filled with freshly prepared food for the agents processing the crime scene.

Dolph was in the base tent, cataloguing more artifacts recovered from the site. He looked up from his laptop when Charlie said, "Hello! Hungry yet?"

"Yes, sir, I am. Can eat only so many peanut butter sandwiches."

"Oh...and that's what I brought," Charlie said sadly.

"Tell me that ain't true!" Dolph cried.

From the open zippered doorway of the tent, Marco said, "That smells more like hamburgers and other good things."

Charlie said, "You're right! I brought you hamburgers, and other assorted delicious items. You should be good for another twenty-four hours at least. So, how goes it here?"

As Marco rummaged through the box of food, he remarked, "This is all homemade! Thank you, Charlie! This is real food."

Dolph whined, "I brought homemade food!"

Marco looked at his partner and said, "Dolph, I'm always glad you bring food. But, no offense, your homemade food is not as...well, as...complex as Charlie's. Look what's in this box!"

Dolph looked in the box and said, "Okay. I see your point. Thanks, Charlie."

"You are both welcome. So, where are things here?" Charlie said.

"We've gathered quite a few personal items from the general area of the graves as well as from the area surrounding the grave sites." Marco said as he enthusiastically ate his hamburger.

Emma said, "Interesting. What kinds of things? May I look at them?"

"Well, a scrap of paper torn from a rental car contract. No name on it, only the rental car agency. And, we found things like a small pocket knife, an empty wallet, a pair of generic reading glasses, along with a small comb. They're all bagged and tagged there on that table."

Emma began going through the labeled zip-lock bags on the table. "You have a lot of personal belongings types of artifacts. How about clothes? We found so many bodies with clothes missing," she said.

Dolph responded, "Five bodies had pants and shirts on. Two bodies were only in underwear. No shoes on any. No other clothes found, except for a couple of ragged deteriorated pieces of t-shirts. It's like they took off their outer clothes, emptied their pockets and fell into their graves."

Emma said, "Interesting. Maybe they did just that."

Charlie was looking at his phone. He said, "Jackson has IDs on two of the victims. One was from Seattle and the other from Cody, Wyoming. Both were white divorced men in their late-fifties. DNA of both was found in CODIS."

"Why were they in CODIS?" Marco asked.

"Health care workers. One was a nurse practitioner,

and the other, a nurse," Charlie said as he continued to scroll his phone. He suddenly looked up and asked Marco, "How am I able to connect to the internet? Service was so bad before."

Marco smiled and replied, "I made the van, its electronics system and the satellite phone, a hot spot. We have a pretty good connection most of the time. Not all the time. It can fade, but it comes back."

"He's good at that sort of make-it-work engineering," Dolph remarked.

"Good. You're not marooned here. You have normal connection with the rest of the world," Charlie said.

"And our pockets are full, and we still have all our clothes!" Marco added.

"Any sign of the shadow cowboy? Or any other phenomenon?" Charlie asked.

"Nope. Except for some animal movements, it was quiet all night. It snowed for a while, but not a whole lot. It was extremely cold just as you predicted," Marco replied.

"Interesting. How do you know they were animal movements and not human?" Emma asked.

"I called out. No one answered. And then the noise of the movement moved away," Dolph said.

Emma said, "Show me where the noises came from."

Emma followed Dolph out of the tent. He led her to the area immediately east of the cemetery site.

Dolph asked her, "What are you going to do?"

"Look for new tracks."

"Want me to go with you?" he asked.

"Probably a good idea. Are you armed?" Emma asked.

"Yes. Always prepared," Dolph replied.

They walked into the forest. Emma searched the ground carefully. The night's snow had filtered through the pine forest canopy leaving a fresh thin layer of white on the forest floor. A short distance into the forest, Emma stopped and pointed to human boot tracks in the new snow. The tracks stopped at a tree and then retreated as they had come.

"Your animal was walking on two feet and wearing boots. Looks like about a men's size ten or eleven," Emma said to Dolph.

"Are we going to follow the tracks?" Dolph asked.

"Yes. Come on," Emma said as she photographed the tracks and walked along side of them.

"This is exciting. I don't get much field work beyond site processing," Dolph told her.

The tracks took a circuitous route east and then north and then west back to the entry road to the cemetery site. At that point they lost the tracks.

"Must have gotten into a vehicle here," Emma said. "Did you hear a vehicle last night?"

"We were listening to some music in the base tent while we catalogued. If it was during that time, we wouldn't have heard it."

"When did you hear the noises? Before or after the music?"

Dolph said, "After. It was when we turned off the music that we heard the noises from the forest."

"What exactly were the noises?"

"The sound of walking on something crackly, like ice, rocks, and sticks," he said.

"Just walking? No running?"

"Just walking."

"Okay. Let's go tell Charlie what we found," Emma said.

When they got back to the base tent, Charlie and Marco

were talking to Jackson via the speakerphone on Charlie's cell.

Charlie said, "Anything from the first batch of artifacts we sent?"

Jackson replied, "Quite a bit of info. The muddy cell phone belonged to a young man from Brooklyn. His family reported he went to New Mexico last summer. He was escaping the pandemic. The lockdown in the spring last year had hit him hard. He lost his business, a small bakery."

"Was he a missing person?" Charlie asked.

"Yes. His family reported him missing when they didn't hear from him for over a month. But the missing person report was only posted in local databases by law enforcement despite the family telling them he'd headed for New Mexico. Apparently law enforcement believed he was a missing-by-choice case."

Emma stepped up to the phone and asked, "Was he one of the victims?"

Jackson replied, "We got DNA from the family. It has been sent to our lab. We'll be able to compare by late today."

Charlie asked, "What about the corn chip package? Any info from that?"

Jackson answered, "The lot number showed us it'd been shipped to and presumed sold in Amarillo. It was from a production lot from a year ago, which corresponded to the expiration date on the bag. We're contacting the vendor in Amarillo, but not expecting great things from that."

"Any other specifics that might help us here?" Charlie asked.

"Autopsies are going quickly. You can retrieve the reports so far completed. I put them in your e-box. Notice there was some fake fur found with/on a couple of the bodies. No fur-ish clothes were found. Also, there are hairs that don't belong to the victims. Those are in analysis now," Jackson said.

"What kind of hairs?" Charlie asked.

"Human. Black and longer than five inches. Most of these black foreign hairs found are consistent with each other. There were other hairs found, but they represent a variety of human hairs from various people, and some animal hair and fur, and none of those are as numerous as the black hairs."

Emma asked, "What is your conclusion from that?"

Jackson said, "That one person with not-short black hair interacted with the victims before or after they were killed."

Charlie asked, "Do you have CODs for any of the victims?"

"Yes. Causes of death are varied. Most were shot in the back, with arrows or bullets. It appears others had blunt force trauma to the head, some from behind and some from the front. We'll know it all when the autopsies are completed."

"Hit in the head from the front? Any defensive signs on the victims."

"No. The pathologist believes the victim was laying down face up when hit across the forehead with something like a pipe or a bat. That victim was hit hard enough to crush the forehead and crack the back of the skull. So the head was not on a pillow."

"Hummm. That's an odd situation. Why wouldn't the victim see it coming and fight back?" Marco asked.

Emma answered, "Asleep or unconscious."

"Or blindfolded, or blind," added Dolph.

Jackson added, "Also, note that the clothes, that were not deteriorated too far, found with the bodies appear to be newish. We could identify many of the clothes as from national sporting goods stores, the big suppliers of hunting and fishing clothes."

Emma said, "I did notice that the bodies still clothed were wearing camo or green or tan heavy canvas pants. Winter outdoor pants."

Marco said, "Yes. That's right. No slacks or blue jeans in the lot."

Dolph said, "So these victims were hunters with new clothes?"

Charlie replied, "Sure could be."

Jackson told Charlie that he'd keep dropping reports into his FBI e-box as the information became available. The call concluded.

Emma and Dolph apprised Charlie of their discovery of the boot tracks in the forest. They showed Charlie the photos.

Charlie said, "Let's get some game cams. We can set them along the route the tracks made. If the intruder returns tonight, maybe we'll get an image."

Dolph asked Charlie, "So, do you think we are in any danger?"

"Probably no more than usual," he replied.

Marco looked at Dolph and asked, "What does that mean? I don't usually think I'm in danger when we're working a scene!"

Charlie laughed, "I don't mean you are in danger. I mean I can't say you're not in danger."

Emma said, "Want me to work with you tonight? I'm happy to come help sift dirt and whatever you need help with. Safety in numbers."

Dolph said, "Sure. We can always use help. This site is fairly large, should take at least two more days to complete."

She said, "Okay. I'll be back tonight about seven. Armed and ready to help."

Charlie said, "Good. Emma will protect you."

On the drive back to Taos, Charlie asked Emma, "You think your husband will mind if you go back up to the crime scene tonight?"

Emma laughed, "He won't mind at all, in fact, Harry might want to come with me."

Charlie said, "That's not a bad idea."

Toady called Charlie from Sheriff Deelly's office in Angel fire. Charlie and Emma were on their way down from the cemetery site.

"Hi. Toady. How was the interview with Kako?" Charlie asked.

"It went well. Maddy and I'd like to debrief you when you have a few minutes," Toady said.

"Meet me at the house in Taos for dinner this evening. I haven't spoken to Sam and Carlos yet. We can go over their info and the data Jackson has sent. Will that work for you and Maddy?"

Toady spoke to Maddy, who was with him at the sheriff's, and said, "Yes. We'll be there. About seven?"

"Perfect. See you then."

Emma took Charlie back to Taos. As he got out of the car, she told Charlie that Harry had game cams. She offered to take a few up to the cemetery and set the trap.

CHAPTER 20

Just as Charlie sat down in the living room and began downloading the reports and data Jackson had left for him, Sam called.

"Hi. Where are you?" Sam asked.

"I'm in Taos at the house. Where are you?" Charlie replied.

"Carlos and I are in Angel Fire. The interview with James Frustini and Susan Mileser also included another local construction guy named Hop Sovern. It was a fruitful visit with them. Right now, we are on our way to have a drink or coffee or something with another person of local color named Steve Smedley. Hop set up the date for us. Steve is another of James' subs. He's a finish carpenter. He has been around here for a number of years," Sam said.

"Where are you meeting him?" Charlie asked.

"At a bar and grill near the slopes. It has an outdoor serving area. Hop said that would be important when meeting with Steve."

"Okay. Hope it goes well. Toady and Maddy are coming here this evening for dinner. You and Carlos should be through by then? Say, by seven? There is a lot of data from Jackson to go over."

"We'll be there. Hop said an interview with Steve should

be a quick one," Sam responded.

"Why?"

"He wasn't clear about that. But Susan said that Steve smells bad."

"Smells bad? What does that mean?"

"I'll let you know. We're on our way over there now. See you later," Sam said.

Sam and Carlos reached the restaurant after Steve Smedley.

The masked woman who stood at the entrance holding menus asked, "How many?"

Carlos said, "Three. We're meeting someone here."

The woman said, "Steve? You're meeting Steve?"

"Yes."

She led them to a table at the far rear of the outdoor seating area, far away from other tables. A late-middle-aged, unmasked man with long stringy black hair and a long beard was sitting at the table eating from the basket of complimentary chips.

The woman handed them menus and retreated.

"Hi. You are Steve?" Sam said.

"Yes I am. And you are the FBI agents?" Steve replied.

"We are. May we join you?"

"Yes. Sit down."

When they were seated, Sam and Carlos removed their masks. They helped themselves to some chips.

"Nice to meet you. Hop tells us you are the best finish carpenter around. Do you have other interests? Jobs?" Carlos began.

A waiter appeared and asked what they wanted.

Sam said, "Can we get something hot to drink? Hot chocolate?"

Steve said, "Me, too."

The waiter nodded and hurried off.

"Start with basic questions: How are you? Where are you from? Things like that," Steve suggested.

"Okay. How are you? Where are you from? Do you live in Angel Fire?" Sam asked.

Steve replied, "I am fine. I was born in Oklahoma City. Lived there until I went into the army. Served enough years to get a small pension and then moved here. I am a carpenter. I live near Angel Fire. How are you? Where are you from? Where do you live?"

Sam smiled at him and replied, "I'm fine. I am from Chicago. I live there, but I travel a lot for work so I am not home very much."

Carlos laughed and said, "What he said."

Steve laughed.

Sam asked, "You said you live near Angel Fire. We are investigating a case near Angel Fire, up in the mountains. On Greg Moranos' land. Where do you live?"

Steve said, "Oh yes, the cemetery that Tibbet found. I live west of there. Not too far. I have forty acres."

"Did you build your house?"

"No. I built my yurt. I'm off-the-grid as they say. All solar. All self-contained."

"What does self-contained mean?"

Steve said, "It means I have everything I need and want."

"Do you grow your food and such?" Carlos asked.

"In season I do garden outside. In the winter I have a few vegetables growing inside. I have a few sheep and goats and chickens. What do you want to ask me about the cemetery?"

"Did you know it was there before Tibbet found it?"

"No."

"Have you been to the cemetery?"

"Yes. I saw it. Had to check it out. Everyone was talking about it."

"Do you have any idea who put it there?" Sam asked.

"No. But I don't think Greg had anything to do with it. He's a nice guy. You ever hear his podcasts?" Steve asked.

"We sat in on a recording session for one just yesterday."

"What'd you think?" Steve asked.

"It was fascinating. Greg has had a lot of experiences that are way out of the ordinary. Nice that he's sharing those experiences. Might help others in some way."

Steve said, "I agree. Greg might help others who have had unexplainable experiences somehow reconcile those experiences."

"Exactly. It can be upsetting to have an experience that doesn't fit any model," Carlos said.

Sam asked Steve, "How did you get to the cemetery?"

"My truck."

Sam clarified, "No, I mean, what route did you take to find the cemetery?"

Steve said, "First I called Artie Tibbets and asked him where it was. He gave me the coordinates. I found it online. The most direct path was from the county road west of Greg's place and then through the forest. I walked the last part from the county road."

"You didn't drive in?"

"Didn't see a road to drive in on," Steve answered.

"What was your impression of the cemetery?" Carlos asked.

"Impression? Well, I thought it was a staged joke or

something," Steve said.

"Why'd you think that?"

Steve said, "The markers, the headstones, looked fake, small, all the same size and color. I've never seen a cemetery like that. Thought maybe some kids set it up to look like a cemetery."

"Real bodies were buried there. Not fake at all," Carlos said.

Sam asked, "Did you walk around the site?"

"Yes. I walked around it, but not through it," Steve said.

"Did you see any of the bones that stuck up through the dirt?"

"I did. Thought they were fake," Steve said.

The waiter brought their hot chocolates and a bill. Sam picked up the bill and said, "It's on us."

Steve sipped his chocolate and said, "Thank you. It's good hot chocolate."

Carlos asked, "Did you touch anything at the cemetery?"

"No."

"There is no record of a legitimate cemetery being there. We are treating it as a crime scene because there is evidence of homicide with the bodies."

Steve said, "With or on the bodies? Which is correct?"

Sam laughed, "Well, there is evidence that the victims buried there were murdered."

"When?" Steve asked.

"That hasn't yet been determined. When we were recovering the bodies, it looked like some had been in the ground longer than others. None of them were buried deep. All shallow graves," Carlos explained.

Steve said, "That's odd, isn't it?"

Sam said, "Yes, kind of odd. But if a killer wanted to make a quick job of the burials, then a shallow grave makes sense."

"Were the victims killed there? Or somewhere else and then moved to the burial site?" Steve asked.

"We think they were killed somewhere else. But that hasn't been determined for sure yet," Carlos said.

"Would you give us the coordinates of your yurt? I'd like to see it. Would that be possible?" Sam asked.

"Sure. No one's ever asked me about it. When do you want to see it?"

"How about late tomorrow morning? We're staying in Taos. It'll take us a little while to get over here, and then we'll have to find your place."

Steve took a small pad of paper from his shirt pocket. He wrote the GPS coordinates for his yurt on the paper and handed it to Sam.

Sam said, "You have the coordinates memorized?"

Steve Smedley answered, "Yes. I have a lot of things memorized."

"I suppose we all do. I have the multiplication tables memorized," Sam said laughing.

Sam asked for Steve's cell number. Steve added that to the piece of paper.

They finished their hot chocolates and said goodbyes.

On the drive back to Taos, despite the cold, Sam and Carlos kept the windows open in the Tahoe.

CHAPTER 21

"Hi there," Carlos said to Toady and Maddy as he and Sam entered the house.

"Hope you guys didn't eat at that bar and grill. Dinner is almost ready," Charlie called from the kitchen.

Carlos said, "No, sir. We stuck to hot chocolate."

Sam said, "Smells great in here! Do we have time to clean up?"

Toady said, "Good idea. No offense, but you two smell more than a bit barnyardy."

Sam said, "I know we do. We met with Steve Smedley. He smells loud and proud like the unwashed, with a few barnyard animals thrown in. We absorbed his aura."

Toady said, "Ha. I've heard that about him."

Sitting down to dinner, everyone was delighted to see Charlie had prepared yet another fabulous meal. This night he'd fixed grilled pork and beef medallions with a cranberry glaze, a mixed green salad, and mashed potatoes with a cheese crust.

"Is there a dessert I should save room for?" Sam asked.

"Yes indeed. A peach crumble with vanilla ice cream."

Toady said, "Charlie, you sure are nice to feed us so lavishly, so beautifully."

Charlie said, "I fix the food I want to eat."

Maddy said, "Thank you for wanting this! Everything is delicious!"

After dinner, they adjourned to the big living room. Carlos stoked the fire in the fireplace. Everyone took a seat and the debriefing began.

Charlie started, "Jackson has sent a lot of info. I'll list the points:

1) Twelve graves, evidence of seven bodies.
2) All males. Ages range from twenties to fifties.
3) CODs are gunshot, and arrow wounds, and also trauma to the head. The deathblows and wounds were delivered to the back of the victims. Except for one, which received a blow to the forehead.
4) Clothes remaining more or less not yet deteriorated were new and outdoor sports type clothing.
5) Grave markers/tombstones were made of a plaster epoxy mix. All from the same mold. It's a mold usually used for pet cemeteries or home pet graves. It's available online.
6) The five digit numbers on some of the grave markers are not part of the mold. They were stamped into the plaster epoxy surface. They might be zip codes.
7) The tire impressions are from a tire consistent with the factory tires used for the past three years on four-wheel drive F150s.
8) Comparing satellite images from the past decade, the cemetery is not visible until five years ago.
9) The cell phone belonged to a man from Brooklyn, NY. Lab is still working on it. We are getting the subpoena for the call records. The fitbit was new

and had not been registered yet. It was bought online by a man in Texas.

IDs are slow in coming. I will prepare a list separately. Now let's breakdown what you all found out today."

Toady said, "Maddy and I met Greg's wife, Kako Williams. She is a beautiful middle-aged woman. A head-turner as they say. Her store is jammed full of stuff. Everything from antique furnishings to clothes and accessories."

Maddy added, "She was friendly, but she had an edge of insincerity."

Carlos asked, "You mean you thought she was lying?"

"She might have been. She was certainly holding back. She's sincere about selling merchandise. But not so much about herself and Greg. Phony is the word I'd use to describe her responses. Kind of like she's playing a part rather than being herself. She made a point of saying Greg is out in left field. She made him out to be a crackpot."

Toady said, "Oh, and also I bought a coat, gloves, and boots from her. I think the FBI lab should examine them. And I got good thumb and forefinger prints on the credit card I used for the purchases."

Charlie asked, "Examine for what?"

"Not sure. I just had a feeling that the hunting or outdoor sports clothes in her shop were somehow out of place. They didn't fit in with the other merchandise. She's a good display artist, and she tried to blend them in, but they still stood out." Toady said.

Carlos said, "Since some of the victims were missing outer clothing and shoes, you might have found something."

Toady replied, "I thought the same. But it might be stretching things to think any missing clothes would end up in a shop right there in Angel Fire."

Charlie said, "Our lab will be able to determine if there's anything to it. Give me the credit card with the print. I'll find out if she's in any of the databases."

Sam asked, "Did Kako seem like the killing type?"

Toady said, "I don't know how to answer that. People can be such chameleons. I've been fooled before."

"Well Steve Smedley is no chameleon. Don't think he could blend in anywhere. Except maybe in the Chicago Stockyards," Sam noted.

CHAPTER 22

The next morning, after careful scrutiny of Google maps, Sam and Carlos felt confident enough to head for Steve Smedley's place outside of Angel Fire. The morning's weather was more wintery than it had been. The temperature had dropped overnight and showed little interest in warming up. Light snow was falling in Taos.

Upon reaching the village of Angel Fire, The snow was falling with more determination. The GPS coordinate destination of Steve's yurt was at the end of a route that included paved roads and various winding and somewhat challenging icy dirt forest roads. Many turns and turn-arounds finally deposited them at an unexpectedly ornate steel gate with the name Smedley emblazoned on it.

"This must be the place," Carlos announced.

Sam stood by the gate and pointed to a chain and lock. "Now what?"

"Let's climb over and hoof it to the yurt," Carlos suggested.

They walked up the slippery steep dirt road beyond the gate. The road wound through a dense pine forest. After about a quarter of a mile, they rounded a turn in the road and saw a large clearing with a yurt as well as fenced pens and several barn-like outbuildings. A white Dodge Ram 3500 diesel was parked by the yurt. They continued towards the yurt.

Carlos called out, "Steve! Hello!"

As they were almost across the clearing, and about fifty feet from the yurt, Steve emerged from the forest to their left. He called out, "Hello FBI!"

It startled them, as they were focused on the yurt and negotiating the snowy clearing.

"Wow. Hi Steve!" Carlos called back.

Sam muttered to Carlos, "Have we lost our mojo? He snuck up on us!"

The two agents met up with Steve just outside the yurt. All three were masked.

"This is much larger than I thought it would be," Carlos said to Steve.

"It's over seven hundred square feet. About a thirty foot diameter. Come in," Steve said as he climbed the freshly shoveled wooden steps to the deck outside the entry door to the yurt.

The yurt was built on a round wooden platform that was four feet above the ground surface. A band of three-foot high, wide vertical boards encircled the lower half of the structure sitting on the platform. Above the wooden band, a brown canvas tent rose vertically another six feet then angled toward the high center crown point of the circular building. The overall effect was of an exotic tent. They entered through a conventional door set in the lower band and upper vertical portion of the tent facing the deck.

"This is quite the surprise to me," Carlos said. "It's so big in here."

The space inside was open with the various use areas set around the perimeter of the large round room. There were two windows and just the one front door. In the center was a wood stove with its smokestack extending all the way to the apex and compression ring of the tent's high ceiling. Though the day was quite cold outside, the interior of the yurt was warm.

"Oh, you have company," Sam remarked when he noticed two goats sitting quietly near the woodstove.

Steve said, "Sam and Carlos meet Alpha and Beta."

"How do you do," Sam said to the goats.

Carlos asked, "Are these goats? Or sheep?"

Steve laughed. He explained, "These are goats. They'll eat anything. And they usually do. They're called browsers. They'll stick their noses into anything and everything. Sheep graze and eat grasses mostly. Goats have hair not wool. If goats have horns like these do, the horns point up and kind of backwards. If sheep have horns, they curl around the side of the head. In addition, sheep tails point down, and goat tails, when the goats are standing, point up. Goat ears are smallish and stick out, as opposed to sheep ears, which are longer and flop downward. It is hard to tell them apart when they are at a distance, but up close they are entirely different."

Sam said, "I see. And if they're in your house, you can see the difference right away."

Steve laughed again and said, "I do have sheep outside. They live in the pen. They have their own house out there."

"Yes, I noticed the outbuildings. Are those the sheep houses?" Carlos asked.

"One is. One is the wood, tool, and storage shed. And one is the chicken coop. Have a seat."

The agents sat at the table near the woodstove. The goats did not stir. Steve made tea in the small kitchen area, and offered them a cup.

"This is nice tea. What kind is it?" Carlos asked.

"It's sage and gingko tea. My own mix," Steve said.

Sam said, "Hmm, both are considered helpful for brain function. Both are supposed to aid in staving off dementia and depression."

Carlos said to Sam, "When did you pick up tea-talk info like that?"

Sam laughed, "I read the labelling at the grocery!"

Steve said, "You're right, Sam. My hope is this tea will help keep my brain at its best as long as possible."

"Life goes by so fast! I agree it's important to be a proper steward of your whole physical self every day," Sam added.

"I see you have running water here. Must have a well. Do you have a septic system? Electricity?" Carlos asked.

Steve explained, "Electricity is solar. I have batteries in a metal storage container under the decking here. My well is on this far side of the yurt from the animal pens. My septic is behind the rear portion. That is the area opposite the door."

"Very impressive setup here," Sam said.

"I don't see a bathroom. Do you have one?" Carlos asked.

Pointing to the area near the bed, Steve said, "Behind that curtain over there is the toilet and small cold tub. No room for a full sized bathroom. No hot water. Maybe next summer I can add that."

"It's so warm in here now. How does this fare in the warmer months?"

Steve responded, "I can open the windows and the breeze sweeps around the space effectively. I can also open the top to let rising heat out. See up there near the stovepipe, that section is zippered. That was my own addition after the first summer here."

"Very cool," Carlos said. "This is quite the home."

"Yes it is. Did you want to ask me more questions about the cemetery?" Steve asked.

"Yes. Can you tell us anything about Greg Moranos, or about Commodore Craymist?

"I've met them both. Though I don't really know them. Craymist is a funny old guy. He likes to present himself as the rich kid on the block. He might be. I don't know. Greg is a good plumber and an interesting, genuine sort. His podcasts are great. I love those."

"I don't see a computer or TV or any electronics in here."

"Everything is in that," Steve said motioning towards a tall beautiful piece of furniture.

"I thought that might be a wardrobe. It's stunning woodwork. Did you build that?" Sam asked.

Steve said, "Yes. I did. Thanks. It's an office and a closet."

Steve opened the door on the closet/office. The interior was a study in efficient use of space. On the left were drawers with hanging rod up top. On the right was a TV on the upper shelf and below was a desk with a fold down work surface. On the inside of the door hung several rifles and a compound bow.

"That is very nicely done! Do you hunt?"

Steve answered, "I eat. So I hunt."

"Do you eat the animals that you keep here?"

"No. I sell the sheep wool and I consume the goat milk and chicken eggs."

Sam said, "Glad to hear you don't consume your roommates."

Steve laughed, "They are my companions. They're very

sweet."

Carlos asked, "Do you know Kako, Greg's wife?"

"I've met her. She seemed to me a bit of a snob, a superficial snob. She is friendly and cordial and all. But, she seems to be putting on. Fake smile."

"Oh. Well, have you ever seen her on the road up to Craymist's place?"

"Nope. Never see anyone much on these roads up here. Not too many people live out this way. Is she under suspicion?" Steve replied.

"No one in particular is of special interest right now. We're just gathering info. Getting to know the people around here. You are so right about there not being many people living in this area. Pretty much just you and Craymist and Greg."

"Craymist said he's had some poachers on his land. Have you had that issue?" Carlos asked.

Steve said, "Not recently. Over the past few years, occasionally I have heard gun shots in the woods. Sounded close enough to be on my land."

Carlos asked, "What'd you do about it?"

"I shot a few rounds into the air to let them know the area was occupied," Steve replied.

Sam asked, "Did that do the trick?"

Steve said, "Yes. Poachers don't want confrontation. And neither do I."

"If you had to guess who might have been responsible for the cemetery and the deaths of the victims buried there, who would you think might be capable?" Sam asked Steve.

Steve thought for a moment, then answered, "Almost anyone I know would be capable. But I really can't think of anyone who would be likely. Angel Fire sees so many visitors every year, all year round. Anyone could have chosen this area for a place to deposit bodies. Anyone who visits here could come back over and over again and raise no suspicion at all. But that location of the cemetery is so remote, I can't imagine some outsider picking it and then getting to it, and with bodies. It's a mystery."

"It is that," agreed Sam. "You're right about the tourists. They do come and go all year. And I know there are many houses and condos that are vacation homes for people from all over."

Steve asked, "Any connections between the victims?"

Carlos said, "We don't know about that yet. We're working on it."

CHAPTER 23

Toady and Maddy found Charlie still at the table eating breakfast. They joined him for coffee and toast.

"No Tahoe in the driveway. Where are Sam and Carlos this morning?" Maddy asked.

"They're up at Steve Smedley's place. I say that with all confidence that they found it! They haven't called, so I guess the adventure is smoothly underway," Charlie replied.

"What do you hear from Jackson?" Toady asked Charlie.

"He has IDs for some of the victims. Every one of them came out here to hunt. They bought hunts for the Timberlake Ranch."

"That's Greg!" Maddy said.

"It is," Charlie responded. "Greg is the only guide who has or has had the lease at that ranch. All of the victims so far identified were clients of his."

Toady said, "Can't imagine Greg as the perp for these killings. It just doesn't fit."

Charlie said, "Jackson is getting background info on both Greg and his wife. We have to know more about them before we talk to them again."

"Ask Jackson to get backgrounds on Steve Smedley and Commodore Craymist, too," Toady requested.

Maddy asked, "Did any of the identified hunters come to New Mexico together?"

"The victims we know about came alone, though they may have been paired with other hunters once here. We'll have to ask Greg how his hunts work. We need to get his client list. We need a lot more info from him."

Maddy asked, "When were the hunts that the victims came for?"

"The families and friends of the identified victims gave us various dates going back five years. The victims were all reported missing persons when they didn't return from New Mexico as scheduled. But, as happens, the missing person reports stayed local to the victims' home town or state. No investigations out here," Charlie reported.

Charlie's cell phone rang. He took the call. His end of the conversation was clipped and sounded serious. When he hung up, he said to Toady and Maddy, "I have to meet Emma at the Taos hospital. Harry was shot, ambushed, with an arrow, early this morning. She is driving him to the hospital. Would you two go up to the cemetery and get statements from Dolph and Marco? Find out exactly what happened. Emma is too upset to be clear right now."

Maddy said, "Oh God! When did this happen?"

Charlie replied, "Sounded like she said it happened at daybreak. She said they were checking the game cams. Didn't see who shot him."

Toady asked, "Where was he hit? How bad is it?"

"Emma said he was hit in the back, but the arrow didn't pass through. Might have hit the scapula. She said they were able to slow the bleeding almost completely and stabilize him somewhat before she and Dolph and Marco got him into her vehicle."

"God. Sure, we'll get up to the site right away. Tell Dolph and Marco to wait there for us. You can take my police SUV. We'll go in Maddy's pickup," Toady said as he and Maddy got up to leave.

"Thanks. I'll call later when I know something," Charlie said as he grabbed his gun and coat.

When Toady and Maddy reached the crime scene, Dolph and Marco were standing by their van.

Toady asked them, "What happened?"

Dolph said, "Harry came with Emma last night. They set six game cams around the perimeter of the site."

"Five," Marco corrected.

"Yes, okay. Five game cams. They helped us in tents #1 and #2, and then in the base tent. You know, photographing, cataloging, bagging, and such. Harry was a big help. He began drafting maps of the site."

Marco said, "It got too late and cold to work anymore, so about ten we turned in. Dolph and I slept in the van, and Emma and Harry slept in the base tent. They brought a little camping tent with them, but the base tent already had cots and a heater set up. So, we gave them that space. The van has a heater and bunks. Then early this morning, I heard them up and about, so Dolph and I got up to help with breakfast."

Dolph then said, 'We offered to fix breakfast. They said they'd go out and check the game cams they'd set up last night. They were gone about twenty minutes when Emma came running back. She said Harry'd been shot. We grabbed the first aid kit and followed her back to where she'd left Harry."

Marco picked up the story, "Harry was lying in the snow on his stomach. An arrow was sticking out of his right upper back. There was a lot of blood. He was conscious. I immediately applied the coagulation compress packs to the wound around the arrow. The broadhead had ripped a bad wound. I asked him if he could move his feet and hands. He could. So I felt the arrow had not hit his spine. He said he was cold. We wrapped him up in a space blanket, except for the arrow sticking out of his back. Dolph ran back to the van and brought a cadaver stretcher. We carried him to Emma's Subaru."

Dolph continued, "Her car was packed with supplies, so I pulled everything out of it. That stuff's all piled up over there. Then we put Harry, still face down, in the car, through the back hatch. Had to lay him at an angle to get the hatch closed. Emma took off for the hospital in Taos."

Toady asked, "Did you hear anything last night or this morning? Anything in the woods? Movement? Were there any lights? Anything?"

Dolph said, "Nope. It seemed quiet to me. Didn't hear anything this morning when he was shot."

Maddy asked, "Have you looked around in the forest since the shooting?"

"No. We've stayed right here. Didn't want to contaminate any evidence. Or get shot."

"Okay. Well, show us where he was when he was shot," Toady requested.

Toady and Maddy followed the two FBI techs into the forest near the cemetery. About thirty feet into the thick trees, they reached the patch of bloodied snow.

"He did lose a lot of blood," Maddy remarked looking at the wide red stain on the snow.

"From what direction did the shot come?" Toady asked.

"From how he was on the ground and what Emma said, I think the shooter was back in there," Marco said pointing into the trees in the direction away from the cemetery.

"Bold. The perp felt safe enough comfortable enough to come back here, even with law enforcement here. Let's spread out and work this scene. Look for any and everything. The perp is cocky. Cocky can lead to mistakes," Toady said.

They carefully fanned out and began a search of the ground, trees, rocks in the area the shot was assumed to have come from. It wasn't long before Maddy yelled out that she found something. The others carefully made their way to her.

"What is it?" Toady asked.

"Look at this," Maddy said. She pointed out fresh-looking boot prints in the snow by a tree. The tracks came from the west, and wandered around through the forest towards the cemetery and back to the tree. The person stood by the tree, then retreated to the west.

"Well let's follow these tracks," Marco said.

Toady said, "You all follow the boot prints. I'm going to continue to look around."

Dolph thoroughly photographed the boot prints as they led them back to the logging road.

"What the hell? The perp drove in on the logging road. Parked, then walked the rest of the way. We never heard a thing," Marco said.

"This is too far away from where we were. We couldn't have heard. We need to check the game cams," Dolph said. "Where are they?"

Marco replied, "I don't know where they put them. We'll have to find them."

They returned to where Harry was shot. They called out for Toady. He came out of the thick forest carrying two game cams.

"I marked where these were, and tagged the GPS. Where are the rest?" Toady asked.

"We don't know."

"These two were very close to this spot. Let's go check them out," Toady suggested.

In the base tent, they put the chips from the two game cams into Dolph's laptop. The images were of no help. They saw only small game and blobs of snow falling from the trees had triggered the motion detectors.

"We have to find the other three cameras. What can we use to do that?" Toady asked the techs.

Dolph thought, then said, "We do have a small Flir with us. Since that will register heat and infrared signatures, maybe it can help us."

"Great. That will spot the infrared light on the game cams if we can trip the motion sensors," Maddy said.

Dolph said, "Our challenge will be to differentiate the small infrared light from the other warm surfaces in the daylight."

"Maybe we'll luck out. It is so cold today."

She and Dolph began a careful sweep of the surrounding forest. Marco and Toady began collecting samples of everything they could find at the spot where Harry fell.

Finally, after a long search, Maddy and Dolph found two more game cams. They brought them back to the base tent. Toady and Marco were there. One of the cameras had captured a figure moving from left to right across the field of vision. It was a human wearing a long coat with a hood. The hood covered the head and obscured the face. On the infrared image the coat appeared light with dark bands across and down the center of the back and encircling the arms just above the wrist.

Dolph said, "Since we're looking at an infrared image, the light color is most likely a dark, and the dark colored striped parts are perhaps dark but of a different material. The stripes could be leather or plastic. The coat could be a fabric. Since the image is probably the perp, I'd imagine he or she is wearing all black or dark brown or dark green. In any event, that's a rather fancy coat."

Maddy asked, "Have you checked in the two tents over the cemetery site this morning?"

Dolph looked at Marco and they both stood up and headed for the other tents. In tent #1 they found all was as they'd left it the night before. But in tent #2, one of the excavated graves in which they'd not found a body was now filled in with dirt. Marco immediately spread a small tarp by the grave and began to slowly scrape aside the fill. Under about eight inches of dirt, he found a body.

"Holy crap!" he exclaimed.

Dolph helped Marco uncover the new body. In a short time they revealed the body of a male dressed in camo cargo pants and a green t-shirt and snow boots. There was an arrow through his neck parallel with his shoulders. Toady recorded the excavation on his cell phone.

"Maddy, that's Deputy Marvin McShine!" Toady said sadly.

"Oh my God!" Maddy said. "I'm going to call Sheriff Deelly and then Charlie. Is there cell service?"

Dolph said, "I have to turn it back on. We're using the van and a satellite phone for a hot spot."

"My God! How bold is this perp? Burying a victim in the tent in the middle of the night and then shooting Harry!" Marco exclaimed. "This is unheard of!"

Toady said, "We are dealing with someone who is out of control."

Maddy asked if she could go ahead and use the satellite phone. Dolph took her to the van and handed her the phone.

She called the Sheriff and then Charlie.

After talking at length with both of them, Maddy returned to tent #2. Toady and the FBI techs had put Deputy McShine's remains in a body bag. They were just about to remove the body bag. Maddy followed them to the van. The men carefully set the bag on the ground under the rear bumper of the van.

"It should stay cold here. We'll get the transport up here right away," Dolph said.

The four of them just stood there staring at the forest. Toady finally asked Maddy what Charlie and Brad had said.

"The sheriff is coming up here. He said dispatch had received a call from a woman late last night. She reported there was a disturbance near Greg Moranos' house. Deputy McShine responded to the call. He radioed in that he was at Greg's house and that all was quiet. That's the last they heard from him. The sheriff thought Marvin had gone on home," Maddy told them.

"How about Charlie?"

Maddy said, "He's at the hospital in Santa Fe with Emma. Harry was sent down there on a life-flight copter. He's in surgery. He will survive. But his right shoulder and right lung are both a mess. Broke a few bones in the shoulder and nipped the top of the lung. The arrow penetrated pretty deeply, but missed the major blood vessels."

"How's Emma?"

"Charlie says she's hopping mad," Maddy said. "And also, he said he left your SUV at the Taos hospital. He drove Emma to Santa Fe in her car."

"I'll bet she's mad!" Toady agreed. "Somebody shot her Harry!"

"We're going to work the site. There may be something of use. It all happened when it was late, dark, and cold. The perp had to have left us something!" Marco said.

Dolph and Marco returned to tent #2. Toady and Maddy wanted to find the fifth game cam, so they resumed the search in the forest. Luck was with them. They found the fifth camera placed in a tree, up higher than they'd found the others. Toady retrieved it and they took it back to the base tent.

The camera had done a good job. It caught the image of the same long coated human figure as seen in the image from the other camera, but this time the figure was not alone. The coated figure was walking behind another figure. The figure in front had no coat, just t-shirt, pants, and boots.

"That's Marvin. Looks like he's being forced to walk in front of the figure wearing the coat," Maddy said.

"He is," Toady said as he watched the clip over and over. "Still can't see the perp. Time stamp shows this was caught just after four AM."

Maddy added, "So the perp killed Marvin and buried his body in tent #2 before shooting Harry at daybreak. Daybreak was about seven."

"That means the perp had a little time between shootings. Wonder what he did." Toady mused.

"Well the other camera caught him at six-thirty-six. That must have been as he was leaving. Maybe the shot taken at Harry was a shot of opportunity. He saw Harry checking cameras and shot him. Then the perp would have hurried away. So the direction he was going in the other image was what?" Maddy said.

Toady brought the previous clip up on the screen. The figure was moving alone and westward. He said, "The perp was walking back toward the logging road. That's his point of entry and exit."

Maddy said, "Smart move. There've been so many

vehicles in and out, it'd be nearly impossible to tell what tire tracks are what."

Sheriff Deelly stepped into the base tent. "Oh my God! Marvin! Where did..?"

"Let me show you," Toady said as he led Sheriff Brad Deelly to tent #2.

Dolph and Marco stood up when the sheriff entered the tent. They'd been sifting through the dirt in and around the grave.

Dolph said, "You have our sincere condolences. This is tragic."

Brad Deelly asked, "When did this happen?"

Toady answered, "From the game cam clip, the perp brought Marvin here around four this morning. The perp marched him here at gunpoint we surmise, though the gun is not visible in the clip. I'll show you the footage. Let's go back to the base tent."

Back at the laptop, Toady queued up the first clip that showed the perp walking behind Marvin. Then the second clip showing the perp walking alone back towards the entry trail.

Brad Deelly said, "I don't recognize the perp or the coat. It does look like Marvin was being forced to walk. And where was his coat? His hat? He would have been wearing his fur hat with the earflaps. It was very cold last night!"

Toady said, "None of the other victims had outer clothes. Marvin is the only one to have his footwear. All the others had no shoes or boots. Marvin wasn't shot in the back. All but one of the other victims were assaulted from behind. He was shot from the side."

"Weapon?" Deelly asked.

"Either a crossbow or a compound bow, using a fixed broadhead. The arrow is still in the body, it went through his neck. We're hoping there are prints on the arrow. Must have been carrying the bow under the long coat since it's not visible in the game cam footage. The perp was more rushed than usual. It was after burying Marvin that the perp encountered Harry in the woods and shot him in the back. We think shooting Harry wasn't planned. But killing Marvin was."

Deelly said, "Damn right it was planned. The asshole enticed Marvin up here or somewhere and took him. Marvin was not an easy target. He was a savvy officer. I wonder if he knew the perp."

CHAPTER 24

Charlie was able to secure a vehicle in Santa Fe, a Chevy pickup, from Agent Peel at the Santa Fe FBI office. Harry was going to be in surgery for a while, so he left Emma at the hospital. Tim Peel assured Charlie that he'd stay with Emma.

When Charlie got back to the house in Taos, Toady and Maddy were there. Colfax County Sheriff Brad Deelly was with them. They were sitting at the dining table looking at Toady's laptop.

"What do you have?" Charlie asked.

Toady related all that they'd discovered so far at the crime scene and cemetery.

"Marvin would not have been taken easily. He had to have known the person who captured him," Deelly noted.

"I'll call Jackson now. We have to accelerate everything we are doing. The perp is in crisis. The danger factor couldn't be higher. We have to have background info on everyone connected to this case. And as soon as we do, we have to interview them. Brad, can we use your office in Angel Fire for the interviews. We'll want these people on our turf for the interviews."

Brad Deelly said, "Yes. Sure. You can use the office and any other resource we have."

Toady suggested, "I'll initiate a trace on the call made to the Colfax County dispatch last night. The call that Marvin responded to."

Charlie went to the living room to call Jackson. He updated Jackson on all the happenings. He stayed on the phone a long time. When the call concluded, he returned to the dining table.

"Jackson had lots of news. Greg Moranos is originally from Santa Barbara, California. He's from a wealthy family there. He graduated from Stanford with a degree in engineering. From her social security number on her business license and fingerprints she left on Toady's credit card, we've determined Kako Williams was originally Maryann Pierce. She was born in Royal Oak, Michigan. That's a suburb of Detroit. Her older brother, Alan Pierce was arrested and indicted, but not convicted for the abduction and murders of at least eight children in the 1980s. It was a notorious case in Michigan. All the children's bodies were found pretty close to each in a small lake in the lake district near Royal Oak. They had all been killed by a blow to the head from behind. They'd all been sexually assaulted post mortem," Charlie began.

Maddy asked, "How old were the victims? Genders?"

Charlie said, "All between eight and twelve. Boys and girls."

"How old was Alan Pierce when the murders occurred? Over what length of time did the murders occur?"

"Pierce was nineteen when arrested. The murders spanned nearly two years. Alan Pierce was ten years older than his sister Maryann. The police determined that Alan had been sexually abusing his sister since she was a small child."

Toady asked, "Why wasn't he convicted?"

"Not enough evidence to convince the jury. It was the eighties. Times were different. And it was in a large population area. If it'd been in a small town, the outcome might have been different. But who knows," Charlie said.

"How'd Maryann Pierce become Kako Williams?" Maddy asked.

"She moved to California possibly right after she turned sixteen. Changed her name, met Greg and married him. Records show she was eighteen when she married Greg. They lived in Santa Barbara for a year. They migrated to Angel Fire twenty-one years ago. She reemerged as a retailer six years ago. The police report from the case in Michigan indicates that she knew what her brother was doing to those children. She may even have played some part in entrapping the victims. Remember she was nine when he was arrested. He was abusing her while killing those other children. She may very well have a fragile and seriously disturbed psyche as a result of her childhood with Alan." Charlie explained.

Toady said, "She may also have followed her brother's example. Let's see if I have this story right. Kako Williams, forty-two year old retail merchant, is really Maryann Pierce, victim and sister of Alan Pierce, child killer. What happened to Alan?"

Charlie said, "He fell off the radar about the time Maryann moved to California. He would have been twenty-eight or twenty-nine when he disappeared. He hasn't surfaced since then."

"Good God!" Sheriff Deelly exclaimed. "Maybe Alan Pierce is dead. Maybe he was killed by a parent of one of those little children he killed!"

"Could be. Could be anything. Today he'd be fifty-two," Charlie noted.

Maddy asked, "What about Greg Moranos made him husband material for Kako?"

Charlie said, "The behaviorists at the Bureau seem to

think Kako would need to have a relationship she could control. Could Kako be the alpha partner in that marriage?"

Toady answered, "Yes she could. Greg is not an alpha sort. She sets the rules for their relationship."

Maddy said, "Let's get her in for a talk."

Charlie said, "Yes. If you and Toady will surprise her with a visit and take her to the sheriff's office, I will get all the info the Bureau has on her and join you. Let me know when you are there."

Toady said, "We'll head over to Angel Fire now. If she was out in the woods last night, maybe she'll be tired enough to tip her hand."

Charlie cautioned, "Don't underestimate her. She has survived a lot in her life. If she is our prep or knows our perp, she's not going to give it up. Be careful."

Sam and Carlos returned from their trip to Steve Smedley's place. They walked in on the serious meeting at the dining table.

"Hi. What's everybody doing here? Whose Chevy pickup is that in the driveway?" Carlos asked.

Charlie told them what had happened at the crime scene and cemetery. He filled them in on Kako Williams' backstory.

"Holy shit! Harry?! Marvin?! What can we do?" Carlos said.

Charlie said, "Toady and Maddy are going to take Kako in for an interview. Brad is letting us use his office for this. I'd like you and Sam to pick up Greg and take him in to the sheriff's office for an interview. Fingerprint and DNA sample them both. Let them know the other is there. But don't let them see or talk to each other. No communication between them. I am going to call Jackson back. Our lab is looking for any DNA or prints or anything on the artifacts that have been collected. Hopefully we will have something to tie someone to the events."

Sam asked, "Any background on Commodore Craymist or Smedley yet?

"Craymist is just exactly what he appears to be, a rich man from Texas who bought that large property a few years ago. He has no shady past that we know about. Don't have Smedley's history yet, but Jackson said within a couple of hours."

"How old is Smedley?" Maddy asked.

Sam said, "Hard to tell, but I'd guess he's in his fifties."

Deelly asked, "Don't you all ask for identification when you talk to people?"

Sam said, "Yes. Most of the time. But the smell factor with Steve is overwhelmingly distracting."

"How was the yurt experience?" Charlie asked.

"Goaty goat goat goat!" Sam said. "Steve Smedley has goats in his yurt! He literally lives with goats, and he doesn't have hot water with which to bathe or clean his clothes."

Carlos added, "And he has sheep and chickens, too. But they don't live in the yurt. It was all kinds of weird. But it was perfectly normal-land for him."

Sam said, "An odd thing to me was that Steve asked us as many questions as we asked him. He asked the kinds of questions an investigator would ask."

Carlos agreed, "Yeah. Steve's sharp."

Sam said, "He bright enough to be a competent perp."

CHAPTER 25

Mid-afternoon brought cold winds and swirling snow to the village of Angel Fire. Toady and Maddy found Kako Williams' Ford F150 parked in front of her store, "For All Time." The door to the store was locked, but the lights were on inside. They knocked on the glass door. Initially no one answered, but after more knocking, they saw Kako approaching the door.

Kako, unmasked, opened the door with a smile and a pleasant, "Officers! Nice to see you. Come in."

Maddy said through her mask, as she and Toady stepped in out of the cold wind, "Hello. Glad we caught you here. We need you to accompany us over to Sheriff Deelly's office for an interview."

Kako asked, still with a smile, "Oh? Why?"

Toady said, "We need to record an official interview with you, and get your fingerprints and a DNA sample. The cemetery and bodies were discovered on your land. It's normal procedure."

Kako looked from one officer to the other, not saying anything. Her smile remained in place. Then she responded, "Well, okay. Let me get my coat and bag."

Maddy accompanied her to the back of the store, to her office. She took her long coat with the fur collar from the coat rack in the office, the same coat Maddy had seen her wearing when they visited her before. Maddy helped Kako put on the big coat.

"How cool, I see your coat has a hood inside, as well as this nice fur collar," Maddy said.

"Thank you," Kako replied simply.

Toady, still wearing his mask, was waiting by the checkout counter. He asked, "Can I get the lights for you?"

Kako stopped mid-step and replied, "No. Greg might be stopping by."

"I don't know how long this will take. Maybe you should close up for the afternoon," Toady suggested.

Kako said smiling, "Okay. I'll get the lights."

She twirled around and headed back towards her office. As she took a step, Maddy turned to join her. Kako unexpectedly pulled a revolver from her coat pocket and threw her arm around Maddy's neck. When Toady realized what was happening, he saw Kako with a chokehold on Maddy and a gun pressed against his partner's head. He reflexively drew his gun.

Kako said, "Don't do that. Don't make me hurt Maddy."

Toady re-holstered his gun. He said, "Maddy, are you okay?"

Maddy whispered through her mask, "Yes."

Kako said, "Not for long unless you both follow my instructions."

Toady said to Kako, "What are you doing? We just want to interview you, get a statement. What precipitated this?"

Kako smiled and said, "Really? Well I don't think that's all you want. You are working with the FBI. They have access to all sorts of databases. I'm not interested in whatever nonsense they've come up with. I've seen how they work."

"Where have you seen how they work?" Toady asked.

"You know very well. I want you to take off your gun and slide it across the floor past me. Then I want you to get her gun and do the same," Kako commanded.

Toady removed his gun from his holster and slid it across the floor by the Kako. He then approached Maddy's right side, and reached for her gun. It was clipped into her holster. He unsnapped it and as he slowly removed it, he shifted his weight, and swiftly kicked Kako square on her left kneecap. She screamed in pain, dropped her revolver, buckled and fell.

Maddy immediately rolled Kako onto her stomach, arrested her, and cuffed her hands behind her back. Toady retrieved the firearms and helped Maddy lift Kako in her long coat to her feet. She said she couldn't stand on her left leg. Toady called for an Angel Fire EMT response team. They helped Kako to a chair where she sat until the EMTs arrived.

Toady met the EMT ambulance outside the store. He gave them a quick synopsis of the situation. The two masked medical technicians entered the store with a gurney in tow, looked at Kako's knee and after securing a brace on the injured leg, took her to the ambulance. They said they'd have to take her to the Taos hospital for x-rays. Maddy rode in the ambulance with them to Taos.

Toady began a search of the store. He also called Charlie and Sheriff Deelly to report the situation.

Charlie said, "Deelly is going to send an officer to help you search the store. He's also getting a search warrant for her house. I'll go over to the hospital and help Maddy."

Charlie got to the hospital right after the ambulance arrived. The emergency room nurse said to him, "You're becoming a regular here, agent."

Charlie said, "Not my intention. How is Officer Maddy

Lucero? Where is she?"

The nurse said, "She's in room one with the prisoner and the techs. We're going to take the prisoner in for x-rays in a few minutes."

Charlie opened the door to room one. Kako was lying on the bed with her hands cuffed in front of her. She was wearing a hospital gown.

Maddy handed Charlie a large blue plastic bag. "Here are her clothes and belongings. The coat will be of interest. Long coat with fur collar and a hood feature tucked inside."

Charlie took the bag. He said hello to Kako. He moved his mask down so she could see his face. He put his mask in place and said, "I don't believe we've had the pleasure. I'm FBI Special Agent Charlie Black. And you are?"

Kako smiled a tight smile and said, "Ms. Williams."

The x-ray showed no bones broken only bruised. Her knee was going to require a brace and physical therapy to restore use of the ligaments that the injury had hyper-extended. It was going to be a painful recovery.

"We'll get you settled in a patient room and then we can conduct the planned interview here," Charlie said to Kako. "Maddy will stay with you until another state police officer can relieve her."

Kako closed her eyes and did not respond.

Charlie left the hospital with the blue plastic bag of Kako's things.

New Mexico State Police Criminal Investigator Toady Mills with the help of a county deputy sent by Sheriff Deelly searched Kako's store. They bagged the hunting and outdoor sportswear and equipment for further investigation by the FBI lab. When they finished at the store, Deelly called and told Toady he had the search warrant for Kako's home by the country club lake.

Toady and the deputy went to Kako's rented home. They had to force the lock to gain entry. Inside, immediately they saw an arsenal of weapons laid out on the dining table. There were four compound bows, two crossbows, two twenty gauge shotguns, four rifles of various calibers, with an assortment of scopes, and four handguns. There was ammunition for all weapons stacked neatly on the dining chairs. In the living room they found laid across the sofa and side chairs an assortment of outdoor winter clothing, footwear, and accessories. On a table in the living room, were wallets, rings, eyeglasses, credit cards, and a lot of cash.

"Holy moly! What is this?" the deputy asked Toady.

Toady replied, "The motherlode of evidence!"

The two law enforcement officers called Charlie and then Sheriff Brad Deelly to report the find. Toady took pictures of everything and sent them to Charlie.

Charlie called Toady, "Guess it's over for her. What about an accomplice? Any indication?"

"Not that I've seen. Haven't gone through everything. But she was definitely in charge of the armory. Going to need another CSI team to process this house."

Charlie said, "Yes. I'll get a team there ASAP. Secure the place, of course. And I'll call Sam and Carlos. They should have gotten Greg to the sheriff's office by now."

CHAPTER 26

FBI Agents Carlos Sanchez and Sam Wester arrived at Greg Moranos' front door at the same time Toady was dropkicking Kako's knee. They donned their masks and knocked on the door.

Greg answered the door promptly, "Hello. Come in. It's way too cold to be out there. It's way too cold to have the door open."

Sam and Carlos stomped their snowy boots on the mat inside the door.

Sam said to Greg, "Hi. We're here to request you come with us to Sheriff Deelly's office for a formal interview regarding the cemetery found on your land."

Greg said, "Okay. When?"

Carlos said, "Now."

"Right now? Okay. Let's go," Greg said amiably as he put on a mask and coat.

The three men rode in the FBI Tahoe down to the village of Angel Fire and the sheriff's office. At the office, the FBI agents fingerprinted Greg and got a DNA swab sample. Then they put Greg in a small interview room. There were four chairs, and a table with a recording device on it. There was an observation two-way mirrored window in the wall next to the door. They were seated at the table with Greg on one side and

Sam and Carlos across from him on the other.

"So let's begin," Carlos said as he initiated the recording with stated date and time, and who was in the room.

Sam asked, "Greg, how did you meet Kako?"

Greg looked a little surprised, but answered, "In Santa Barbara years ago. I'd have to calculate what year it was if that's important. She and I were at a restaurant on Sterns Wharf. We were each there alone, at one of those places where you sit outside overlooking the harbor, almost sitting right over the water. Someone walking behind me jostled me and I spilled my beer and some of it spilled onto her leg. I apologized and she said it was okay. That's how we met."

"You are from Santa Barbara aren't you?" Carlos asked.

'Yes. My family was there."

"You still have family there?"

"My parents are gone now. My sister lives in Maine. I haven't been to Santa Barbara since my mother's funeral. And that was twelve years ago, I think."

"Did you know Kako's family?"

"She wasn't from there. No I never met any of her family. She was estranged from her parents and she said she was an only child."

"Where did she say she was from?" Sam asked.

Greg answered, "Florida. She said that she and her parents had never gotten along well and then they joined some religious cult-like group. She left."

"Have you ever heard of Alan Pierce?" Carlos asked.

Greg thought and then said, "No. Who is he?"

"He is or maybe was Kako's brother. Kako's real name is Maryann Pierce. Her brother was a serial child-killer in Michigan, in the 1980s."

"Wait! What?! No I never heard about that," Greg exclaimed. "So her brother was caught?"

"Yes he was caught but not convicted. The prosecution was unable to present enough convincing evidence for the jury. Reasonable doubt won out. Then Alan disappeared in the nineties. He vanished."

"How many children did he kill? He's still out there, somewhere?" Greg asked.

"Eight bodies were recovered. We don't know if he's alive or dead," Carlos said.

"What? God! No, Kako never mentioned any of this," Greg said.

Sam excused himself to take a call as he looked at the screen of his ringing cell phone. Once outside the room, he tapped the phone and said, "Hey, Charlie."

Sam listened for a few minutes then said goodbye to Charlie and returned to the interview room.

"Greg, have you ever been to Kako's house here, you know, by the lake?" Sam asked.

"No. She's never let me go there. She always comes to my house," Greg replied.

Sam asked, "Do you know her friends? Who does she hang out with?"

"She is friends with Susan Mileser, and she has her customers that she's friends with. I don't know of anyone else in particular. She has a pretty good customer base here in Angel Fire. Well, before the pandemic. Now she has her store online. That keeps her busy. She doesn't really hang out that I know of," Greg said.

Carlos asked, "Greg, how do your clients get to Timberlake Ranch?"

Greg answered, "Oh, several ways. Some drive here and

I meet them in the village and they follow me to the Ranch. It's a drive. All the way over towards Las Vegas, New Mexico and then back towards Ocate. Or, they fly in to Albuquerque or Taos and take a shuttle to the airport in Angel Fire. Kako meets them at the Angel Fire airport. She takes them to her store where she'll have a rental car for them. She gives them a map and they drive to the ranch. Or, I pick them up at the airport. Or, if they have their own plane they can fly directly to the ranch. There's a nice landing strip and hanger there."

Sam said, "The victims from the cemetery on your land, the ones who have been identified, had all purchased hunts with you. Have you ever had clients go missing?"

Greg replied, "What? No, well yes. That is, sometimes I have no-shows."

Sam asked, "What do you do about no-shows? Do you contact them?"

Greg said, "I send an email to them. I verify the dates that were booked and ask if they'd like to reschedule."

Sam asked, "Do they usually respond to your email?"

"Not always. But usually they let me know ahead of time if they are not going to make it."

Sam asked, "What about those who don't let you know ahead of time or respond to your email? Do you pursue the matter? Do you refund any payments?"

Greg answered, "If a client doesn't respond to me, and never shows up for the scheduled hunt. I don't chase them down. Any deposits made, I keep until I'm asked to refund them. Everyone is told from the beginning that cancellations within a week of the hunt are non-refundable. But I only ask for half down and the other half when they arrive."

Sam asked, "Can you supply us with your client lists for the past five years? And tell us which of those clients was a no-show, and never cancelled or got in touch with you?"

Greg said, "Sure. I have it all in a database."

Carlos asked, "Why do you think a hunter would pay the deposit and then not show up or cancel?"

"I don't know. Could be they or someone in their family got sick or had an accident. I always suspected that they just changed their minds," Greg said.

"But wouldn't they want their money back?" Carlos pressed.

Greg said, "I would. But, some of these hunters are first-timers, might be reluctant to ask for a refund. You never know. Sometimes clients are going hunting to piss off a spouse. Maybe they told their spouse they were going hunting but really were going somewhere else to rendezvous with someone else."

"Has any law enforcement agency or anyone ever contacted you about any missing hunters?" Sam asked.

"Yes. Families have emailed to ask if the client ever showed up. I have responded to every inquiry. All I can tell them is that the person never showed up."

Carlos asked, "How many no-shows do you think you've had in the past five years?"

Greg thought about it and then replied, "Not many really. I'd guess less than ten."

Sam asked, "How many hunters do you average per year?"

Greg said, "I plan for fifty or so, max, per year. I have tags to buy ahead of time and that's the total. There are various kinds and lengths of hunts at different times of the year."

"What kinds of hunts do you mean?"

"Different animals to hunt. Elk. Deer. Bear. Lion. Bighorn. Sometimes exotics if they are around. The animals are free-range. Timberlake Ranch isn't a high-fenced animal compound. The animals migrate and breed as they normally do. The ranch is fifty thousand acres," Greg explained.

"What's a high-fenced animal compound?" Carlos asked.

"It's a ranch that is enclosed by a fence high enough, or thought to be high enough to contain deer and other bounding game. They like to call themselves game preserves. But, since they sell hunts, they are not really preserves. Often those ranches are breeding game for trophy hunters. I, personally, think that's just not right. It becomes hard on the species and it is unfair to the animals. It becomes a fish-in-a-barrel hunt. That's not right," Greg said.

"I see what you mean," Carlos said.

Sam asked Greg, "Would you be surprised to learn that Kako had a stash of many kinds of weapons, guns and bows, and ammo at her house?"

Greg replied, "She is a hunter. She has a couple guns and bows."

Sam said, "Would she have fourteen or fifteen guns and bows?"

"Probably not that many. More like a couple of rifles and a crossbow and a compound bow," Greg replied. "She does buy and sell stuff on her online store."

"But she doesn't have a license to sell firearms."

Greg agreed, "No she doesn't have one. She's never mentioned to me that she buys or sells guns."

"Okay. Back to her identity. Do you remember if she ever had any ongoing communication with anyone? Maybe letters or email? Maybe even phone calls?"

Greg said, "Sure. She has communications to and from her customers all the time."

Carlos said, "Any of those seem different to you in any

way?"

"I really didn't and don't pay much attention to her day-to-day activities. She and I live separate lives. We have for many years now."

"Why are you still married?"

Greg said, "I really don't know. I've asked her if she'd like a divorce. I've asked many times. She always says we'll talk about it later."

"Okay. Greg, I want to send a deputy to your house to get a copy of your client database. We're not quite through here. We have more questions. Know that when we are through here, you are not to leave Colfax County until we say you can."

"Sure. I never go anywhere anyway," Greg said.

CHAPTER 27

Officer Maddy Lucero sat across the room from Kako Williams' bed at the Taos hospital. The doctor had given Kako a sedative and pain killer of some kind. Kako had been peacefully sleeping for over an hour when the door opened and a tall man with silver hair wearing a mask and a long dark red thermal coat stepped into the room.

Maddy stood and motioned for him to move out into the hall. When they were out in the hall, she introduced herself and asked him for some identification.

He said, "Sure, officer. Oh, my license is out in my truck."

"What's your name? Where do you live?" Maddy asked him.

"Bernard Young. I live in Angel Fire."

"Why are you here?"

Bernard Young said, "Sheriff Deelly told me that Kako Williams was over here at the hospital. He said there'd been some trouble at her store with the police. Is she hurt bad?"

Maddy asked, "Why did the sheriff contact you about this? What is your concern?"

Young replied, "He didn't contact me. I heard the call for the EMTs, on the scanner. I called the sheriff. I know Kako. I guess you'd say I am a friend of hers. I shop at her store, occasionally. I just came to check on her."

Maddy said, "Long way to come from Angel Fire to Taos in this weather just to check on her. You a good friend of hers?"

"Not really a good friend. Just know her. I've shopped at her store."

"What do you do for a living, Mr. Young?"

"I'm a ski instructor in Angel Fire."

She said, "Well, Ms. Williams is asleep right now. And she is in police custody. You cannot see her."

"Police custody? For what?" he asked.

"I cannot go into that with you at this time. You can check with the FBI agent."

Young exclaimed, "FBI? What does the FBI have to do with this?"

Maddy reiterated, "Like I said, you can query the FBI agent about the matter."

"Where is the FBI agent? Who is the agent?" he asked.

"He'll be here shortly. Special Agent Charlie Black. If you will leave your phone number, I'll ask him to call you."

Young gave Maddy his phone number and left.

Maddy called Charlie, "Where are you? Odd thing just happened. A man from Angel Fire named Bernard Young just came to visit Kako. He drove all the way ovcr from Angel Fire just to check on her."

"I'm on my way back to the house here in Taos. Delivered the bag of Kako's clothes and things to the airport. They're on their way to the lab in Albuquerque. Why'd he come to see Kako?" Charlie asked.

"Don't know. He said he was a friend of hers but not a good friend. I told him he couldn't see her. Told him he'd have to talk to you."

"Okay, I'll call him."

"Are you coming back over here to the hospital?" Maddy asked him.

"I was going to join Sam and Carlos interviewing Greg. They've taken him to Deelly's office. But now I think I should join you at the hospital and see what we can get from Ms. Williams," Charlie said.

"I'm ready for a break. Been a long short day! When will my relief be here?" Maddy asked.

"I understand your office here in Taos is sending an officer right now. Didn't get a name."

"Okay. Should I wait for you? You want me here when you talk to her?" Maddy asked.

"If you can stand it. Yes, I'd like you to. Why don't you go eat when your relief gets there. Then I'll call you when I get to the hospital" Charlie suggested.

"Oh. here comes my replacement. I'll go get something to eat and come back. Is half hour okay?" Maddy asked.

"Oh sure, an hour is fine. I have phone calls to make. See you soon."

Maddy recognized the uniformed officer and so filled Officer Karmer Benalf in on the situation.

"She's asleep right now, or she was. Sit in the room and make sure no one comes in. She is not to see or talk to anyone other than the nurse or the doctor. And if they talk to her. You take note of what is said," Maddy instructed.

The young officer said, "Yes, ma'am. I understand. Is she restrained?"

"Yes. She's cuffed to the bed. Do not go near her. If she needs anything, call the attending nurse or doctor. Don't talk to her," Maddy emphasized. "FBI Special Agent Black will be here soon."

"Yes, ma'am."

"I need to borrow your unit. I'm going to go get something to eat. Won't be gone long. May I have your keys?" Maddy asked Benalf.

"Sure, here you go." He handed her the keys to his police vehicle.

Maddy opened the door to the room. Kako was still sleeping. She motioned to the young officer to go in and sit. He did.

Charlie sat in the living room of the Taos house to call Jackson. He'd already told Jackson about Kako Williams' attack on Maddy and Toady and that Kako was now at the Taos hospital. He wanted to find out more about her visitor, Bernard Young.

Jackson said, "I need more than a name. Did Maddy get a driver's license?"

Charlie asked, "Don't think she did. Just a phone number. We'll have to find him. Any info regarding the arms found at Kako's house? Toady said he'd sent you the serial numbers."

Jackson said, "Yes. The guns all belonged to victims. We have all the IDs now. Every one of them was scheduled for a hunt with Moranos. It makes no sense that Moranos was killing his clients and giving the guns to Kako. I think you should look at it the other way around. Kako as the killer. She could shanghai them, take the guns, and other hunting equipment and clothing and sell it on her website or in her store."

"That's what Toady and Maddy said. Kako's the perp. But why? When and how did she maneuver the victims so she could kill and rob them, and then bury them way up in the mountains?" Charlie questioned.

Jackson said, "Sam sent a county deputy to Greg's

house to retrieve his client database. I got it just a little while ago. So far, I can tell you the victims all travelled alone to Angel Fire. Kako was the only one involved in, or was supposedly involved in, getting each to Timberlake Ranch. Greg was to meet them at the ranch. The victims never arrived for their scheduled hunts."

"Okay. I'm going over to the Taos hospital to interview Kako. I'll send you the recording when I'm finished. How's Harry doing? Have you heard?" Charlie asked.

Jackson said, "He's out of the initial surgery. He'll need more later. He's stabilized and should eventually recover. It's just going to take time. A lot of time. Emma is still at the Santa Fe hospital with him. Tim Peel is there, too."

"Okay. Thanks. I'll call Emma next."

As Charlie clicked off the call and headed to the kitchen for some coffee, a familiar smell wafted into the room. He looked towards the kitchen and saw the beautiful cobalt blue light begin to form out of thin air. He heard his name.

"Charlie! Good to see you," Burkie said as he stepped out of the blue light.

"Burkie, hello. I was just going to get some coffee. Would you like a cup?"

Burkie said, "No. Thanks though. Can we sit in the kitchen for a few minutes?"

"Sure. How are you?" Charlie asked casually.

"I'm fine. I am here to give you a heads-up."

"I could use anything you have to offer!" Charlie said.

Burkie nodded and sat at the dining table. Charlie poured himself a cup of coffee from the thermal pot of the morning's brew.

"Is that still drinkable?" Burkie asked with a smile.

"I'll let you know." Charlie took a sip. Poured it out and

started a new brew.

Burkie said, "A lot is going on with your case. So many innocent victims of an uneasy and anxious energy. The energy responsible has no compunction about killing. This energy needs to kill. I'm sure you can tell that much. But I'm here to warn you that this energy has now turned a corner, so to speak, and is terrified and paranoid. We all feel it."

Charlie responded, "Okay. Are you saying the perp is scared? And who are the 'we' of whom you speak?"

Burkie smiled, "The 'we' is, as always, the others like me. We feel the actions from all sorts of sources in the universe. When some particular energy source or sources emanate destructive or evil intent, we know it. We don't have access to details of the physical, but we do know the state of the energy. We can sometimes pinpoint the source sometimes we cannot. I can't tell you exactly who or where this energy that you are dealing with is. It is close and dangerous. I can tell you it has markedly increased in its intensity and aggressiveness, if you will."

"A heightened state of turmoil?"

"Yes," Burkie said. "Be careful. And caution your people to be on alert. This energy is exhibiting a growing panic. It seems to be on the verge of sudden eruption. It has resources to use to further the destruction. It is not on its own, but it is in command."

Charlie saw the coffee was ready. He poured a new cup. He turned to ask Burkie if he'd now like some, but Burkie was standing in the blue light again.

Burkie said, "Be careful."

At once, the cobalt blue light engulfed Burkie and took him wherever it always does. All that lingered was the calming and comforting aroma that Burkie always brings with him.

Charlie sat down at the table, drank his coffee, and considered everything Burkie had just said to him. He was suddenly struck with the thought that he'd better get over to the Taos hospital.

He turned into the hospital parking lot just as Maddy did. He saw her in the New Mexico state police cruiser. They walked into the hospital together.

Charlie asked her, "You get something to eat?"

"Yes. Hamburger. Drive through. Makes me nervous to get food from any restaurant. Don't know who's in the kitchen breathing, coughing, handling my food. Are they vaccinated? Are they masked and gloved? Are they being careful? Life is not easy in this stupid pandemic world!" Maddy said in exasperation.

"So true," agreed Charlie. "How'd that visitor, Bernard Young, get into the hospital?" he asked as they made their way through the tight security protocol at the hospital entrance.

They showed their identifications and badges to get past the armed guards and metal detectors. The hospital was not allowing visitors due to Covid restrictions, so only authorized personnel were allowed in.

Maddy said, "I don't know how he got in. He didn't have his license with him. Said it was in his truck. Couldn't have gotten in with or without ID if he wasn't somehow authorized. I will have Officer Benalf find out."

"Who?" Charlie asked.

"My relief. He's watching Kako."

They went straight to Kako's room. When they got there, the hall door was closed and the hall was empty. Maddy pushed the door and entered the room. The first thing she saw was Officer Benalf on the floor with his head lying in a pool of blood. She turned to the bed and saw Kako Williams' head was bloodied and bent oddly to one side.

Charlie checked on Kako. She was dead. Maddy knelt down by Benalf, felt his neck for a pulse.

"He's alive," she said. She grabbed a towel from the bedside stand and applied pressure to his head wound.

Charlie quickly checked the bathroom and closet. Then he ran down the hall for help. In moments, medical personnel filled the room. Maddy and Charlie stepped out into the hall and waited. Charlie called Jackson.

"We will need all of the security footage from all the cameras here at the hospital inside and out. This just happened within the past forty-five minutes or so," he told Jackson.

"No problem. I'll take care of it. How was Williams killed? Could you tell?" Jackson replied.

"From the brief look I got, she was bashed over the head with something heavy and short. Like a tool or a pipe. As soon as the doctors get Officer Benalf stabilized and into another room, I'll get back in there. I told them to leave Kako as she is. Need yet another CSI team here right now."

"Already texted for them. We'll divert the team from Kako's house for now. Give them thirty or forty minutes to get there. We can send another team from Albuquerque to work her house," Jackson assured him.

"There was no indication that Kako was any kind of target. We didn't even know very much about her connection to this whole mess. The perp is really in extreme panic mode. He or she came into this hospital which is basically in lockdown from Covid restrictions. There are strict protocols imposed here. We'll find out how the perp got in," Charlie said.

When Charlie clicked off his call with Jackson he heard Maddy on her phone reporting to Toady what had happened. When she concluded that call she told Charlie that she'd reported the incident to the state police office, and that other officers were on their way.

Medical personnel rolled a gurney into the room. Within a minute, Officer Benalf was rolled out and down the hall with nurses hurrying alongside holding the IV drips attached to him. They told Maddy and Charlie that they'd secured his wound and were taking him for a quick X-ray, and then to a room. They reported that he was stable and would probably be fully conscious soon.

Charlie asked Maddy to stay at the door to Kako's room. "We need to be sure no one messes with this scene. The perp must be frantic to have risked coming in here. Hopefully there is evidence. Would you recognize Bernard Young if you saw him again?" Charlie asked her.

"He was masked. No I don't think there was anything outstanding about him. He was about six feet tall. Silver hair. He had no particular accent. He was wearing a long insulated winter coat, dark red. He said he's a ski instructor."

Charlie said, "With people masked and bundled for the cold, it is nearly impossible to get descriptions or recognize anyone. I'm going to the security office. Jackson's warrant for the camera recordings should be coming through shortly. Call me if anything comes up."

It took a while to find anyone with the authority to release the surveillance footage, even with a warrant. Only the tech supervisor knew how to access the recordings. She told Charlie the cameras ran all of the time. The images were preserved on-site for a week before being condensed and archived in the cloud. Charlie gave her an email address at the FBI to upload the files to. He stood by her side while she did it. He then asked her to run the current day's footage from each camera on her large monitor. Charlie and the technician sat at her desk and watched as each camera was displayed.

A camera just outside the emergency room entrance showed a dark blue pickup truck slowly roll by under the entry portico three times in a period of a few minutes. The driver seemed to be checking for something. The license plate was not visible from the camera's position. They checked the same time period on all the other outdoor cameras.

A camera mounted on the building, pointed at the parking lot across from the main entrance, caught a good image of the same dark blue pickup truck as it parked at the end of a row near the building. A man wearing a mask and a long dark coat got out of the truck and walked around to the side of the building rather than towards the main entrance.

The tech switched to the camera on that side of the building. There was a loading dock on that side. They saw a medical supply truck backed up to the dock and goods were being unloaded. There were several men moving carts from the truck into the building. Everyone was masked, wearing a coat, and busy. It was cold and windy, light snow was blowing. No one moved slowly in that weather. The man in the long coat walked quickly into the building. No one stopped him. No one seemed to take notice of him at all.

The tech said to Charlie, "Chink in the armor."

Charlie replied, "Fatal chink."

From camera to camera, they were able to follow the coated man through the hospital. His route was circuitous and taken at a leisurely pace. He nodded at everyone he passed. He, and everyone else, was masked and appeared to be very involved in some task or another. No one stopped him despite the fact that he was the only one walking the halls wearing an overcoat. All others were in hospital uniforms of one kind or another. They all had ID badges on lanyards. His coat obscured any visible ID, if he had any.

"He was noticed and not noticed," the tech said. "No one could have known at a glance if he was an intruder. How could an intruder have gotten past security at the entrance? Clever."

"Right you are. He was either very clever or very lucky," Charlie agreed.

CHAPTER 28

Sam and Carlos were getting ready to take Greg back to his house. But, they were still at the sheriff's office in Angel Fire when Charlie called with news of what had happened at the hospital in Taos. Sam took the call outside the interview room.

"Good lord! Send any images you have of the perp. We'll have Greg take a look. Might get lucky. How's the officer doing?" Sam asked.

"Officer Benalf is groggy, says it happened very quickly. A man wearing something long and dark and a mask burst into the room and charged him as he stood up. He didn't see anything. He has many stiches in his head and a terrible headache. But he's alive and will recover," Charlie reported.

"Did Kako fight back?" Sam asked.

"No. She was asleep."

"I'll tell Greg. Maybe he'll recognize the perp," Sam said.

Sam waited a couple of minutes until the email from Charlie with the images from the hospital cameras downloaded. He scrolled through the recordings. He returned to the interview. Carlos and Greg were talking about podcasting. They stopped talking and looked at Sam.

"What is it?" Carlos asked.

Sam sat down and said to Greg Moranos, "I'm sorry to report to you that your wife has been killed. A man got past security at the hospital and into her room. He hit the state police officer on duty on the head with something heavy. Then he hit Kako with the same weapon we believe. She died instantly. The officer survived and will recover. I am so sorry."

Greg put his head in his hands. He was silent.

Carlos asked Sam, "Was Maddy the officer? Any idea who did it?"

Sam replied, "Maddy was not there. It was Officer Benalf. Charlie sent the images captured by the hospital security cameras. Greg, will you look at them with us. Maybe you'll recognize the perpetrator."

Carlos set his tablet on the table. Sam sent the images to him. The three men watched the footage.

Sam asked, "Greg, do you see anything familiar about the man in the long coat? How about the truck? Do you recognize it?"

"No. But I don't know many people here. You should show this to James and Susan. They know everybody," Greg replied.

"The man got into the hospital and somehow found the room. He encountered Maddy before she went to lunch. Then as we saw in the video, he wandered around the hospital for almost a half hour. He wasn't confronted by anyone during that time. He returned to the room after Maddy left. He put the police guard down, and killed Kako, then casually walked out of the front door of the building. A brazen killer. Does the behavior remind you of anyone?" Sam said to Greg.

"It reminds me of Kako. She'd be that brazen, that sure of herself," Greg said in a quiet voice.

Carlos said he'd take the video to James and Susan

as Greg had suggested. Sam and Greg stayed at the sheriff's office.

"One or the other of them is usually at their office. It's just behind the market," Greg said as Carlos was leaving.

On his way to the Frustini Construction office, Carlos called Charlie. He asked Charlie to tell him everything that had happened and what was known about the perp. Charlie told him about the conversation Maddy had with the coated man.

Susan was at the construction company office. Carlos told her what had happened. Susan said James was out at a job site but should be back soon.

"May I show you the surveillance video from the hospital? Maybe you'll be able to identify the man," Carlos said as he put his tablet on her desk.

They watched the video. Carlos explained to her what she was seeing.

Susan said, "Unusual coat. Not rare, but not the usual coat for guys to wear around here. More like a coat a visitor would wear. The hair looks kinda familiar. But lots of guys have silver hair. And the truck is a common one. Looks like a Chevy. A newer one. Is that blue or black?"

"Dark blue if the camera is accurate. It really could be either. Tell me, what activity would a coat like that likely be used for?"

Susan said, "Well, I think it'd be easier to say what it wouldn't be used for. Not for skiing. If he told Officer Lucero that he was a ski instructor, I'd say that's probably not true. Ski instructors like the short coats and they wear them everywhere. They have identifying patches on them. The instructors have a certain vanity about their positions. They don't go incognito."

Carlos smiled and said, "I see. Okay. Have you seen that kind of coat on anyone you know?"

"Uh, I don't remember seeing it. If a guy is gonna wear a long coat, it is probably going to be black or brown. You know, guy colors. Colors seem to be extremely important to them. I know James would never wear a long burgundy colored coat. Not in a million years. It's just the way they are," Susan said with a slight laugh.

"What wouldn't I wear in a million years?" James Frustini said as he entered the office from the back rooms.

"Where'd you come from?" Carlos said, somewhat startled.

James said, "Came in the back door. Had to bring in a couple of boxes of plumbing parts."

Susan said, "Carlos has some bad news. Kako was killed over in Taos at the hospital."

"What?? Kako was killed? How? What happened?" James said as he removed his coat and put on a mask.

Carlos explained what happened and why he was there. James sat down by Susan's desk with them to view the camera footage. Again, Carlos narrated the videos. James watched without saying anything.

"Do you recognize anything about that man or his truck?" Carlos asked.

James looked at Susan and said, "That sure looks like Hop to me."

Carlos asked, "Your subcontractor Hop?"

CHAPTER 29

"Yes, James Frustini says the man walks like and moves like, has hair like Hop Sovern. Hop is a construction sub. Drywall, roofing, various general skills. Not licensed in anything," Carlos reported to Charlie by phone.

"Find this Hop Sovern."

"On it. I'll have to pick up Sam at Deelly's office. Take Greg back to his house. Then I can head for Hop's house."

"Leave Greg at the sheriff's. Deelly can take him home. You and Sam go find Hop's house," Charlie instructed.

Carlos said, "On my way. James drew a map for me. Pretty sure we can find it quickly enough. Can you get a warrant to search his house for the coat or anything?"

"I'll see what Jackson can do. An ID just on the iffy say-so of one person is kind of thin. How sure was James?" Charlie asked.

"I think it was a solid recognition."

"Does the truck match?"

"James said that Hop has a couple of trucks but usually drives a white Ford. I'll call when we know more."

Charlie said, "Caution. If he is our killer, he is probably on the verge of a melt-down. You and Sam watch out for each other."

Carlos said, "That's our usual MO!"

Carlos and Sam found Hop Sovern's house without much trouble. The weather was once again deteriorating quickly as the afternoon slipped away. It was still light, but barely, when the FBI Tahoe stopped in front of Hop's house. There was a white Ford F350 parked in front of the door.

Sam waited near the Tahoe while Carlos knocked on the door. The house was lit by a single light in a front room. No one answered the door. Carlos called Charlie.

"Do we have a search warrant?"

Charlie said, "No. What about the truck?"

"No. There's a white Ford. No dark truck. Can we enter the house?" Carlos asked.

"Only if there is probable cause. Check all around the outside. Then call me back. I'll call Jackson again," Charlie said.

Carlos and Sam walked the perimeter of the house. It was still under construction. The back of the house was partially built, framed and roofed, but walls not closed in yet, open to the elements. They entered that section. From the framing and utilities in place, they could tell it was a bedroom and bath. The door from that area to the closed in front of the house was hung but no handle or lock. Carlos pushed the door slightly and it opened.

Sam called out, "Hello? Mr. Sovern? FBI."

The agents, with guns drawn and mag lights on, entered the structure. No one was there. They re-holstered their weapons and began looking around without opening anything. They really didn't have to open anything. A table made from a full sheet of plywood resting on two sawhorses held more rifles and bows than were found at Kako's house. Sam photographed everything with close-up shots of all serial numbers. He sent them immediately to Charlie. In the kitchen on the large island were boxes of ammunition, broadheads, and arrows. In the front room, a living room, was a couch piled high with winter coats and shirts. On the floor were pairs of boots of all kinds.

"What is this?" Carlos asked quietly.

"I'd say it was booty," Sam whispered back to him.

Carlos said, "Should we go outside and wait for Hop to come home?"

Sam said, "I think after Charlie sees all of these pics, he will send some backup if he hasn't already. We should get out of here and wait at a distance. I don't want to scare this guy off, before we can have a chat with him."

Sam and Carlos parked their Tahoe in the trees well back down the only road to the house. They waited. It was dark and very cold. The snow began falling in earnest. When Sam's complaining about the cold got annoying enough, Carlos started the engine and ran the heater for a bit. They continued their surveillance for several hours. Hop never showed up.

They called Charlie. "Where is our boy?" Carlos asked the speakerphone in the Tahoe.

Charlie replied, "No sign of him. We have everyone looking for him. His driver's license photo is not a very good one. Full beard and longish disheveled hair. But it's all we have. He left no fingerprints in the hospital room. I have a warrant for his house. So you can go back there and search it. Get some DNA and prints if possible. There are two agents from Santa Fe on their way to you now. You can leave them there or stay with them. Someone has to wait there. I want any prints emailed right away and DNA to our lab in Albuquerque ASAP."

"We're on it, boss. Any ideas as to the motive for all of this?" Sam asked.

"Maybe it has to do with Kako. We know from James and Susan that Hop was somewhat enamored with her. Maybe there was an outlaw relationship between them. Or maybe they just wanted to rob the hunters," Charlie suggested.

"Two weirds in a pod," Sam said.

"Speaking of pods, do you think our podcaster is involved?" Carlos asked.

Charlie said, "I listened to your interview with him today. I think he was in the dark about Kako and the killings."

"We're in the dark and the cold. We'll head on back to Hop's house. Maybe he left some snacks. I'm hungry," Sam said.

Charlie said, "I'll tell the agents to bring you something. Be careful. Hop could be anywhere."

Carlos added, "Yeah. Anywhere doing anything."

CHAPTER 30

FBI Agent Tim Peel had been waiting with Emma Spruce in Harry's room at the Santa Fe hospital since the previous day. It was now dinnertime, again. Tim offered to fetch something.

Emma said, "That'd be great. I don't want to leave. Harry might wake up."

Agent Peel said, "The doc said they put him in a temporary coma. He should be quiet for some time yet. But I understand. If he did wake up alone, that'd be horrible. What do you want to eat?"

"A salad with lots of avocado, cheese, and tomato, please."

Tim smiled and said he knew just the place near the plaza. "It should take me no more than an hour to get it and get back. See you soon."

Emma sat and stared at Harry. He looked peaceful despite the many tubes and machines he was tethered to and surrounded by. Her phone vibrated. It was Charlie calling. She took the call in the hall outside the room. Charlie summarized everything that'd happened in Taos and Angel Fire in the past twenty-four hours.

Emma said, "God almighty! What is this about?"

Charlie said, "We'll know more soon. Sam and Carlos are gathering prints and info from Sovern's house. That will help. Still no sign of him. I'm sending all of this info to Tim Peel. He'll have the Taos hospital's security videos and Sovern's picture from his New Mexico driver's license. He'll show it to you. Call me if anything registers with you."

Emma said, "He's gone to pick up dinner for us."

"I know. I just spoke with him. We don't know where Sovern is. I want you and Tim to be aware that the man is extremely dangerous. He is a live wire. If by some remote chance, he comes there, don't confront him. Defend yourself and Harry, but don't confront him."

"Do you think he'd come here? Why?" Emma asked.

"I don't know what his endgame is. I don't know his motivation. I don't know what to expect. So, expect the unexpected," Charlie said.

"Okay. Tim will be back soon. We'll be okay. No one's getting to Harry."

Tim returned and brought the salads. They were just as ordered. He and Emma sat in Harry's room and ate quietly.

Charlie called Tim again. "Tim, if the perp does show up there, don't let Emma kill him. I know she wants to."

Tim said, "I can tell. I'll keep an eye on things. I put another agent at the front entrance."

Charlie said, "Good. This perp is having some kind of psychotic break."

Tim responded, "Then I hope we can capture him here at the hospital. They have a good psyche ward here."

CHAPTER 31

Carlos called Charlie, "Any results from the prints?"

Charlie replied, "I was about to call you. Yes. The Bureau checked and doubled checked. The prints belong to two people with three identities. Kako Williams, aka Maryann Pierce, and someone else. If it's Alan Pierce, he may very well be Hop Sovern."

"Wait. Hop Sovern is Alan Pierce the child killer from Michigan from the eighties?" Carlos exclaimed.

Sam heard what Carlos said. He took the phone from Carlos and tapped speakerphone. "What?"

Charlie said, "Alan Pierce may be alive and leaving fingerprints in Hop Sovern's house. We are having trouble getting Alan Pierce's prints from Michigan. The DNA should confirm if Sovern is Pierce since we have Kako's DNA."

Sam said, "Thank you for sending backup so fast. We put them to use. We sent an agent with Hop's toothbrush, hairbrush, and unwashed dishes and utensils from the kitchen to the Angel Fire airport. An FBI jet is airborne as we speak. The ABQ lab should have the DNA shortly. Also, the CSI team got here about a half hour ago. So what's next?"

"We will move forward carefully. We keep looking for Alan or Hop. Whoever it is, he will show himself. He's crashing. He's killed Kako. My suspicion is he wanted to silence her.

She'd kept his secrets all these years, but maybe he no longer trusted her," Charlie said.

"Is Greg in danger?" Sam asked.

"He may be. If it is Alan, and he thinks his sister told Greg about him, then Greg could be perceived as a liability. You two go to Greg's house and warn him about his brother-in-law. Stay there and protect him," Charlie directed.

"Okay. We're on our way. Please keep us informed. We'll leave these guys here to finish working Hop's house."

Sam called Greg on the way to his house. "Hi, Greg. Carlos and I are on the way to your place. Should be there before long. This weather is making the roads a bit dicey, so might take us a little extra time. We have news for you."

Greg Moranos said, "Fine. I'm home."

As the agents ascended the road towards Greg's house, they noticed recent tire tracks in the snow. They slowed as they got closer to the turn off to the house. Carlos cut the headlights. The snow was bright enough to delineate the driveway. They turned into Greg's driveway. The winding drive was icy and snow packed, but it was clear that some vehicle had recently driven the same path. They could see the lights from Greg's house peeking through the trees.

Carlos said as he motioned in front of them, "The other vehicle turned into the woods just there."

Sam said, "We should stop here."

Carlos stopped the Tahoe and the agents got out. With guns drawn, they walked close to the edge of the drive, right up next to the trees. As they got to the point where the other vehicle had turned into the trees, they saw illuminated by the lights from the house filtered through the forest, a white Ram 3500 truck parked nose first in the thick forest.

Sam whispered to Carlos, "That looks like Steve

Smedley's truck."

Carlos said, "I don't smell him."

"Because I took a bath," a voice from the trees next to them said.

"Holy shit!" Carlos exclaimed as he physically jumped.

Sam took a deep breath and said, "Steve!? What the fuck are you doing here?"

The three men stood in the near-dark forest with their handguns pointed at each other.

Steve whispered, "Shhhh. Don't shoot me. I'm on your side."

Sam said, "What do you mean? Who are you? What are you doing?"

"Sorry guys, I'm Trooper Steve Smedley with the Michigan State Police. I'm after Alan Pierce. We've been after him for years. Tracked his sister to northern New Mexico some years ago. I resettled here to keep an eye on her. She was our only lead. I know you are after him, too."

"Do you have some ID?" asked Carlos.

"Yes. Here," Steve said as he handed his ID and badge to Carlos.

Carlos read the ID with his small flashlight. "Sure enough. Trooper Smedley looks for real."

Sam asked, "So, Steve, is Hop Sovern really Alan Pierce? And is he here?"

Steve said, "I don't know if Hop is Alan. He doesn't look like Alan, well like Allan looked when he was nineteen."

"We're thinking he is. We just came from his house. It's full of firearms, bows, ammo, etc. All the items a bad guy needs. It is a bigger collection than we found at Kako's house. And the prints in the house all belonged to Kako, aka Maryann Pierce, and one other person," Sam explained.

Carlos asked, "Why are you here now, Steve?"

Trooper Smedley replied, "I heard about Kako being arrested and taken to the hospital. Then I heard she'd been murdered at the hospital. I knew her brother had to be involved if not the perp himself. If he killed his sister, then he has snapped. He's liable to do anything. I thought Greg might be next."

"How did you hear about Kako?" Sam asked.

"Heard most of it on the scanner chatter. Called an EMT I know, and he told me what had happened."

Carlos said, "It's too cold. We need to act, go see Greg, or go sit in the Tahoe."

Trooper Smedley said, "I think you should continue as you'd planned. You are here to see Greg, aren't you? Is he expecting you?"

Sam said, "Yes. We called him. We should go on up to the house. You coming with us?"

Smedley replied, "No. I'll continue surveillance out here."

"Aren't you freezing?" Sam asked.

"No. This coverall is well insulated and has heat packs. I'll be out here somewhere. If you need backup, yell. I'll hear you. Just don't shoot me."

"Okay. You have a cell with you? Give me the number," Sam said. He put the number in his phone.

"Be careful," Steve cautioned. "This man is crazy and angry at the world. He was that way when he was a teenager, and I suspect he is only worse now."

"Roger that," Carlos said.

He and Sam made their way through the trees towards the house. When they reached the steps to the porch, they stopped. They could see Greg through the window to the left of the front door. He was standing by the large dining table. He was staring towards the far end of the room towards the fireplace.

"What's he doing?" Sam whispered.

"Let's see. Let's go around to the back deck. I think we'll be able to see in," Carlos whispered.

They silently stole around to the back of the house. They could see a man standing in front of the fireplace. It was Hop Sovern. He was holding a cross bow, and the bow was pointed at Greg. They could see that the two men were talking.

"What now?" Carlos whispered to Sam.

"We can't jeopardize Greg's safety. Maybe we can lure Hop outside," Sam whispered.

"How?"

"A diversion. Let's be a UAP or an alien," Sam whispered.

"Again, how?"

"I'll be back. Going to get some flares and stuff from the Tahoe. Keep an eye on things," Sam whispered. "Don't let him shoot Greg."

"Oh, Okay," Carlos whispered.

Sam quietly hurried away to get the supplies he thought would work. On his way to the Tahoe, Steve appeared noiselessly from the trees. He fell in beside Sam. Sam was again startled by the stealth Steve displayed.

"Where are you going?" Steve asked.

"We saw him. Hop's in the house. He and Greg are talking. Hop is holding a crossbow on him. I'm going to create a distraction. Going to get flares and lights from the SUV," Sam explained breathlessly.

"You think Hop won't just shoot Greg?" Steve asked.

"If we just bust in, I know he'll shoot Greg," Sam said.

"Why not shoot Hop, from outside, through a window. If you can see him, you can shoot him," Steve said.

"Rather not kill him unless necessary. Rather capture him," Sam said.

"But you can't let him kill Greg," Steve added.

Sam said, "I don't know why he hasn't already. What are they discussing?"

"Okay. Can I help you with your distraction plan?"

"Yes. The Tahoe is just there. Let's get the stuff."

Sam and Steve collected the flare kit, a box of candles, a coil of rope, and two very powerful flashlights. They also found a small propane camp heater with a bottle of gas.

"This'll do it," Sam said.

They quickly and quietly returned to the back deck of the house. Carlos reported that Hop and Greg were now seated at opposite ends of the table. Hop had put the crossbow on the table. It wasn't pointed at Greg any longer.

The three men had a quick huddle, then they began assembling the diversion. The flare kit held ten flares and two flare guns. Carlos removed the gas bottle from the camp heater and set it by a railing post on the deck. Sam and Steve made fuses from the rope by wiping it with a candle. Sam positioned the gas bottle upside down and fed a fuse into its opening, making an effective bomb. Carlos tied four flares together with waxed rope and placed them near the bottled gas bomb.

"All set. Let's do this," Sam said.

Sam, Carlos, and Steve moved away from the incendiary items. Carlos had one flare gun and three flares, and Sam had the same. Sam told Carlos to light the fuses. As a fuse burned towards the gas bottle, and a fuse burned towards the bundle of flares, Sam and Carlos prepared to fire flares.

Just as the gas bottle exploded and the bundle of flares shot in all directions, Sam and Carlos added to the frenzy of noise and light with their flare guns. Sam shot one flare through the window on the kitchen door.

Steve was watching Greg and Hop through a window. Greg jumped up and headed straight for the damaged back door. He threw open the door and ran outside. Hop ran behind him. Hop was not holding the crossbow. He held a semi-automatic handgun.

Steve shined both powerful flashlights in Hop's face.

Sam shot his last flare at Hop's legs. Hop went down with his pants on fire.

Carlos ran to Hop, stomped out the flames, and kicked the gun from Hop's hand. Sam went to Greg who was kneeling by the edge of the deck.

Greg asked, "What happened?"

"UDP. Unidentified Deck Phenomenon," Sam said as he helped Greg to his feet.

Steve helped Carlos move Hop into the house. They lay Hop on the floor in the kitchen with his hands cuffed behind him. Greg sat down at the table where he'd been just before the UDP. Sam gave him a glass of water. Carlos called Charlie and requested an ambulance.

CHAPTER 32

There had never been so much activity at Greg's house, ever. It took almost an hour for the ambulance to get up to the house. The EMTs and a sheriff's deputy were on board. They secured Hop Sovern to a gurney and took him to the hospital in Taos.

Charlie came from Taos. Maddy and Toady showed up, too. Greg was still a little shaky, but was doing fine. They all sat at the big dining table. Sam introduced Trooper Smedley to the FBI agents and to Greg.

"My god, what a night!" Greg said.

Sam explained the diversion they'd created and the subsequent mayhem that led to Hop's burned pants and arrest.

Charlie said, "Good work! What made you think to create a UDP?"

Sam said, "Greg. He has seen so many unidentifiable phenomenon here and on his deck, I was counting on him to want to investigate. He surpassed my expectations. He just flew out of the kitchen to see what was going on."

Carlos continued, "That made Hop chase after him. Steve blinded Hop with the flashlights, Sam knocked him down with a flare to the legs. And that was that."

Trooper Smedley asked Charlie, "They told me the DNA

analysis…"

Charlie said, "Don't have results yet. But I'd be surprised if Hop's DNA wasn't Alan Pierce's DNA. We'll know tomorrow I hope."

Toady asked Steve, "How long have you been undercover on this case?"

Steve answered, "Pretty much since Alan Pierce disappeared. Decades now. We couldn't give up. What he did to those children was horrible. I followed Maryann to California, then followed her new identity of Kako Williams here to Angel Fire. I have been relieved a few times over the years by other troopers. But, I am so glad I am here now. I'd have hated to have missed the finale!"

"What made you think Alan was still alive? That Kako would lead you to him?" Maddy asked.

"We didn't know. But she was our only link. The parents both died shortly after Alan was first arrested. Car accident. Car went into Lake Erie. We always thought Alan had something to do with that, but couldn't prove it," Steve explained.

Sam asked, "How and why did you come up with the stinky subcontractor cover?"

Steve laughed and said, "I'd done it in California, and it worked great. Nobody looks too carefully at someone who smells really bad. They just want to get away. Easy enough to keep an eye on things when no one will stay close to you."

Sam asked, "How did you stand it? The smell."

"It is true that you can get used to any smell," the trooper replied. "And I really like my goats and sheep."

Charlie said, "You are a dedicated lawman!"

Toady asked, "So, Hop was the man who killed all of those victims in the cemetery?"

Charlie said, "Looks like it. We'll get a statement from

him I hope." He asked Greg, "That coat by your fireplace is his?"

Greg replied, "Yes. He took it off and left it there. Kinda hot standing by the fire."

"It looks like the coat in the video from the game cam by the cemetery and on the video from the hospital surveillance," Maddy said.

"But what was Hop's motive for all of this killing?" Carlos asked.

Trooper Smedley answered, "He's been on the run all of his adult life. That had to have taken a toll on his psyche. He held only his sister in his confidence. I think that secret-keeping affected her, too. They just crumbled from the psychological strain. Killing was his life. She took the victims' possessions and resold them, I think because she could. He is a disturbed, evil man. He is also a very smart man."

"He is one of those psychos who can seem to fit in with everyone else. Scary to think they walk among us," Carlos said.

"Yes. Chameleons," Sam added.

Greg asked, "Why did Kako marry me? What was she doing?"

Charlie said, "Consensus from the FBI behaviorists is that she wanted further cover. You are from a respected, wealthy family. She wooed you for your normal life."

Greg laughed, "Guess they haven't heard my podcasts. Not such a normal life."

"Hope we didn't scare off any of your unexplained visitors with the commotion tonight," Sam said with a laugh.

"I imagine they enjoyed it," Greg said.

Carlos asked Greg, "What were you and Hop discussing?"

Greg smiled, "Kako. I think he was in love with her. He talked on and on about how pretty and smart she was. I just let him talk. I had no idea where anything was leading. Thank you all for coming to my rescue!"

"You did really well tonight," Sam said.

"More results from Jackson today?" Carlos asked.

"Who is Jackson?" Smedley asked.

"Special Agent-in-Charge of the Dallas Division of the FBI," Carlos said.

Charlie said, "Yes, the belt buckle found under one of the victims at the cemetery belonged to a rodeo cowboy from Oklahoma."

Maddy said, "Shadow cowboy!"

Charlie said, "Makes sense."

"Shadow cowboy?" Smedley asked.

They told the trooper about the 3-D scan images, and the ghostly shadow recorded.

Charlie continued, "Also found from Kako's credit card history that she bought the headstone kits. We think she was hand-in-glove involved with her brother in the killings and the cemetery burials. They went to elaborate lengths to dispose of their victims. It remains a mystery why."

Trooper Smedley said, "Alan Pierce's victims in the 1980s were each ceremonially wrapped in crisp new white sheets before being put into the water. We thought that he and his sister did it together. But, we didn't have all the science available now. We couldn't prove it to the satisfaction of a jury."

"I didn't read that in the reports of the court case," Charlie said.

"I don't think it was in the reports. We held that back in hopes that it would prove valuable later," Smedley said. "Well,

I'd better be going. I have to report this evening's progress to my office in Michigan."

Everyone said goodbye to him. Steve Smedley left Greg's house.

CHAPTER 33

Maddy, Toady, Sam, Carlos, Charlie, and Greg sat at Greg's big table and rehashed the day. Charlie's phone vibrated. It was Jackson. He took the call in the kitchen. After a few minutes, he returned to the table.

"Hop is not Alan Pierce. The DNA doesn't match. Hop is, however, closely related to Alan Pierce. The prints in Hop's house are all Kako's and Hop's, and Hop's don't match Alan Pierce," Charlie began.

Sam interrupted, "Hop is not Alan Pierce? Where is Alan Pierce? Is he alive? How is Hop related to Pierce?"

Charlie said, "Correct. Hop Sovern is not Alan Pierce. We don't know if Hop Sovern is his real name. We do know Hop is a first cousin to Alan."

Carlos said, "So, we start all over again."

Toady said, "What about Hop Sovern? He's gone to the Taos hospital. He needs to be under guard."

"Yes. Jackson sent two agents. Hop's being treated for minor burns on his legs. He'll be released to FBI custody when he is stabilized. He'll be taken to Albuquerque and locked up," Charlie said. "But the most troubling news is that there is no Michigan Trooper Steve Smedley. Michigan has not kept the Pierce case open. Steve Smedley is a fake."

"Then who is Smedley?" Toady asked.

"Maybe Pierce," Charlie muttered. "Maddy would you go to the Taos hospital to help with the security. Don't let Smedley get to Sovern."

Maddy said, "Sure. I'll call in additional officers. They can get there immediately. We'll have state police and FBI. He'll be secured."

Charlie said, "It appears Smedley could be Alan Pierce, but we've made that kind of mistake already. We don't know who Smedley is or why he created the charade of being a Michigan trooper. Maybe he's another cousin. If Kako was killed to keep her quiet, then wouldn't Hop be a liability too? Why didn't Smedley kill Hop tonight?"

Sam said, "In our defense, we didn't have any cause to doubt Smedley, in the dark in the forest the ID looked real."

Charlie said to Sam, "Not to worry. I know."

Charlie called Tim Peel. "Tim, this matter has developed too quickly. We still have a dangerous loose end."

Charlie explained the night's arrest of Hop Sovern and Steve Smedley's trooper con.

Agent Peel said, "I'll call in a couple of additional agents. Can have them here within the half hour."

"Good. This lunatic is smart and has some kind of agenda. Though…I don't know what it is," Charlie said.

Toady asked, "Smedley left abruptly. He has to be up to something tonight."

Charlie said, "If he hasn't simply fled the area, I can think of three destinations that Smedley might be aiming for now. Hop at the Taos hospital, or Harry at the Santa Fe hospital, or the cemetery. Toady, you, Sam, Carlos, and I are going to the cemetery. Right now. Sam and Carlos you take the Tahoe. Stop well before the crime scene. If Smedley is there, we have to surprise him or Dolph and Marco could be hurt. Toady, you come with me."

Greg asked, "Do you want to take the four-wheelers?"

"No, thanks. Too noisy and too dangerous in this weather," Charlie said.

Greg remained at his table. He hoped he'd have an ordinary unexplained paranormal visitor.

CHAPTER 34

Sam and Carlos got to the logging road turnoff before Charlie and Toady. Sam pulled the Tahoe as deep into the snowy forest as he could. Charlie and Toady arrived in the FBI pickup Charlie was driving and pulled in near the Tahoe. The four men met quickly before they fanned out on foot towards the cemetery site.

As they got close, they saw the CSI van, then the base tent, and the two tents over the gravesites. All three white tents were lit within and glowing in the gently falling snow. They saw shadows of movement within the base tent.

Charlie and Toady approached the van carefully, after clearing it, they moved to the base tent. They heard voices from within the tent.

Charlie whispered to Toady, "That's Smedley's voice."

Toady nodded. They very slowly and quietly moved to the door side of the tent, staying about fifteen feet away from the tent. The door's zipper fastening was closed. They couldn't see inside. They waited. The voices sounded calm and friendly, but they couldn't discern the words.

After a few cold minutes, the tent door was unzipped. Dolph stepped out, followed by Marco, then Smedley holding a pistol at their backs. Charlie and Toady backed further into the darkness of the trees.

Smedley said, "You guys have done a great job here. Really gotten into the details of things. Show me the graves."

Dolph said, "Alright. But why? The graves are empty. We're almost done with the investigation."

As the men walked through the accumulated and falling snow, they slipped and struggled to keep their footing. They stepped into tent #1. Dolph was told to zip the door closed. Charlie and Toady inched closer to #1.

Now they could hear the exchange in the tent.

Smedley said, "You have undone everything I did here."

"We just did our jobs. This was a crime scene after all," Marco said.

"Everything here was so well done. The graves. The markers. However, I will admit that Kako picked rather steep terrain for our project. Nevertheless, it did have charm to it. A nice cemetery. It was rewarding to fill it up," Smedley said.

"How did you pick your, uh, people for the cemetery?" Dolph asked.

"Glad you asked. That's a funny story. Kako's husband is an outfitter, a guide. He takes people hunting. What we learned was the newbies travelling alone are too gullible for their own good. They bought new clothes and weapons for their trip. The bought whatever the salespeople at the outfitter stores told them they'd need. Way too much stuff! And, they'd do whatever Kako told them to. They thought they were up here to sight their guns and bows. They found out they were up here to be laid to rest. Now, you boys can be the first to repopulate this cemetery," Smedley said in his calm voice.

"Why was Kako killed?" Dolph asked.

"Cousin Hop believed his perceived girlfriend had turned on him, that she was going to turn him in. He's paranoid that way. He's not very bright. He did a lot of killing for her. Mostly Kako used him. He was her slave," Smedley replied with a laugh.

Marco asked, "What started you in this line of work?"

Smedley replied, "Stalling? Think your fellow agents will come to your aid? Not a chance. Ha! They think they got their man tonight."

"Then, indulge me, why did you take this particular path in life?"

"I like it. It is thrilling as hell to watch death take hold of a person. The moment is incomparable to anything else. It happens in a millisecond of time and is permanent. That is hard to beat," Smedley explained.

"I was told you killed children in the 1980s. Is that true?" Marco asked.

Smedley laughed and said, "I did a phenomenal job, even at that age. Was not convicted. Kako was with me every step of the way. She was very young but she was fascinated with death. We had a good time. When she was old enough, we resumed our projects. We were able to set up small cemeteries in Arizona and Idaho."

Dolph asked, "Were those ever found? Those cemeteries?"

Smedley said, "Oh no. We were very professional. After that period, we made the decision to expand our horizons. She found Greg. He had money and that certainly helped. Then Kako had the brilliant idea to resell the clothes and possessions that otherwise would just rot in the ground. This project proved to be a prototype that we planned to improve and expand upon."

Marco asked, "Tell me, we're thinking…the five digit numbers on the headstones…were those zip codes?"

Smedley laughed, "Yes! That was my idea. Each person's

home zip code. Clever wasn't it?"

Marco agreed, "Very."

Smedley asked abruptly in a tenuous voice, "What was that? Did you see that?"

"What?" Marco asked.

"That black thing. It was right there in the corner."

Dolph and Marco looked behind them to the back corner of tent #1.

"I don't see anything," Marco reported.

"What did it look like?" Dolph asked.

"Like a man. Looked like a man wearing a hat. It was solid, solid black. It moved too quickly. It was right there, inside this tent!" Smedley insisted, suddenly nervous.

Marco said, "Don't worry. It might be one of the shadow people. They won't hurt you."

"Shadow people? What the hell are you talking about?" Smedley said in a shaky voice.

"You know, ghosts," Dolph said.

"Don't be stupid. No such thing," Smedley said. He was visibly sweating.

"I beg to differ," Marco said. "We've been working crime scenes for years now. Crime scenes usually involve deaths. We've seen many lingering spirits."

"Is that true?" Smedley asked Dolph.

"It is. Spirits who have left their physical bodies can sometimes hang around where they died. They just come and go randomly. Nothing to worry about," Dolph assured him.

They could see that Steve Smedley was, for some reason, seriously shaken by this revelation. Smedley sat down on a small canvas campstool left next to a grave. He stared into the open empty grave.

"Is something wrong?" Marco asked him.

Smedley didn't answer. He suddenly jumped up. He screamed and shot at the back corner of the tent. He shot until he emptied the gun. Dolph saw the slide lock open on the pistol. He stepped forward and took hold of the barrel and removed the gun from Smedley's hand.

"Just sit down, Steve," Dolph said.

Marco unzipped the door and stepped out. He took a deep breath. Then he screamed. Charlie and Toady had moved out of the shadows.

"Jeez. You two scared me to death!" Marco said.

"Well, glad it wasn't 'to death,'" Charlie said.

Toady went into the tent, arrested and cuffed Steve Smedley.

CHAPTER 35

Charlie called Jackson to report the arrest of Alan Pierce, aka Steve Smedley. Sam and Carlos came running when they heard the rapid gunfire in tent #1.

"Holy shit! What happened?" Carlos asked when he saw Smedley sitting on a campstool with his hands cuffed behind him.

"We captured a very notorious serial killer," Dolph stated flatly.

Toady said to Sam and Carlos, "Who knew the infamous Alan Pierce was so neurotic? Smart move to make the shadow person in the tent. How'd you do that from outside the tent? Flashlight?"

"Do what?" Sam asked.

"Make a shadow figure appear in the tent. It put the fear of ghosts in old Alan," Toady said laughing.

"We didn't do anything. We were on the other side of tent #2. In fact, we were cooking up a diversion. We were going to ignite tent #2."

Charlie said, "Glad you didn't have to. It was shadow cowboy who took care of things. I think he wanted some justice."

"Well he got it!" Dolph said. "I recorded everything Smedley said. Have my cell phone in my shirt pocket."

"The real Michigan state police will be happy to have the confession, if for no other reason than to put the case to rest. But the Arizona and Idaho agencies will be faced with a difficult task. They'll have to trace Kako's movements in the effort to find those cemeteries Pierce mentioned," Toady commented.

Smedley looked up and asked, "Is it true what you said about ghosts?"

Dolph answered him, "Yes it is. Energy transitions, it doesn't die. It simply leaves the body."

"That is what has been chasing me all these years. I can't stand it. It's terrifying," Smedley said quietly.

"Haunting admission," Sam said.

Sam and Carlos took the prisoner straight to Albuquerque.

Charlie and Toady stayed at the cemetery to get the rest of the details from Dolph and Marco.

"Was Pierce here long? He left Greg's house maybe a half hour before we did," Charlie asked. "What happened?"

Marco explained, "Pierce showed up while we were working in the base tent. We were at our laptops when he just walked in. The door was unzipped but closed. He certainly surprised us. He pulled a pistol on us. Right away he started talking. He described what had happened at Greg's. Then he rambled on about how smart he was to fool the FBI. He told us he wasn't a Michigan trooper. He thought it was exceptionally funny that everyone fell for his story. He told us, in confidence, that he was really Alan Pierce the serial killer who got away with murder in Michigan long ago."

Dolph continued, "He talked about his sister as if she was still alive and then about her being dead. He said he couldn't do without her and then that he was better off without her now. He changed subjects constantly and seem to confuse himself. We recognized that he was having a psychotic break. We kept him talking."

"You did the right thing. I suspect he's been on a downward slide for some time," Charlie said.

Dolph said, "What's that noise?"

Marco listened and said, "Sounds like a high pitched magnetic motor. You leave something on in the van?"

They left the tent, headed for the van.

Charlie said, "Hey. Look at that!"

Looking up they all saw a dimly glowing object in the shape of an open triangle in the sky. It was at least the size of the CSI van. The object gave off a soft intense pink light. It hovered and swayed about two hundred feet above them. It blinked twice and moved slowly towards Greg's house.

The end

cigars with his buddies. He'd argued with her daily about the wonderful virtues of cigarettes and cigars. He always fell back on his inane belief that, "They wouldn't sell things to us that are bad for us!"

Really.

Her job had been for thirty some odd years a pharmaceutical salesperson. It had served her well. She and her two children were among the rich and elite of her town. She measured the elite by wealth. She was living a very comfortable life. Her home was a mansion on the medium sized lake. Only the richest people lived on her side of the lake.

Her son and daughter had gone to the big name state school. She believed her son was now the vice-president of a locally owned bank. Her daughter had served in the Army after college. She believed her daughter was now a state lobbyist for the largest manufacturer of snack foods in the country. Both of her children had homes on her side of the lake, though they used their homes as vacation homes.

At the beginning of her career selling pharmaceuticals she was on the road a lot. Her geographical region was fairly large, but not as large as some. She made it back to her home nearly every sales night. Many salespeople in that industry just stayed on the road all week, paying visits to doctors and hospitals in one town after another. She'd maneuvered her region to the area surrounding her home, keeping a doable radius for daily travel time.

She had moved up the ladder to the position of a regional manager of other salespeople, or drug reps as they were being referred to now. Her job still occasionally took her out of town to various hospitals and large clinics in her sales region. She'd seen the changes in all facets of the medical industry over the years.

When she started, selling pharmaceuticals to hospitals, clinics, and doctors was a straightforward slam-dunk process. There really weren't that many different drugs to sell. Now, however, it was a whole different supply of what could be described, she

Here is an excerpt from another book by Lucinda Johnson:

DOWN then GONE

A Novel by Lucinda E Johnson

CHAPTER 1
the problem at the boat dock

It had been her town for so long. She didn't think anyone could care about her town any more than she did. She'd been born there, grew up there, went to school there, at least through high school. She moved away to go to college, but she'd returned to her town after those four ordinary college years. She loved her town.

Everything in her life was so middling, in every way. Medium sized. Average economy, all around mediocre future for Gray Hills itself. Her family was unremarkable. She'd married an average guy she'd known since childhood. His mother had decided they'd be a good match. So they married. She'd had mediocre sex with him twice. They had two medium children, a boy and a girl. No extremes.

But now her little world seemed to be changing. Her life seemed to be changing. She didn't like that. Not at all.

Now in her fifties, she was still working because her average husband had died of lung cancer when her children were still in grammar school, or grade school as it is ordinarily referred to now. He'd been a three pack a day smoker, and the weekend thought, as a cornucopia of redundant drugs for which advertising and salespeople had to create a demand. That really wasn't a hard thing to do. Humans like new things.

She was diligent about keeping her vast trove of sample drugs locked up. She had a huge, heavy duty gun safe in her home that served as her vault for the samples. She knew better than to believe any hype about any new drug. She was not at all enticed whatsoever to indulge. She found the drug industry to be, simply put, a smarmy self-serving unconscionable monster.

She'd worked for that monstrous industry for a long time, but she had never felt part of it. She had to support herself. She had to.

Gray Hills, as a centrally located accessible mediocre town in the southern Rockies, had served her well. But now there were more people squeezing into the area. There were more people on the planet than ever before. Why did they have to come to her town? She didn't like it.

She liked to walk her side of her lake in the mornings. She'd been instrumental in creating a walking and bike path on her side of the lake. She never saw any reason for people on her side to walk or bike on the opposite side. So, the walking path was truncated at either end of the area she considered her side of the lake. Made perfect sense.

This morning she took her usual path from her back patio down the stone steps leading to the walking path. She always turned right and first walked to the end of the path in that direction. She'd graciously paid for the installation of a grand gazebo at that end of the path. She could see her beautiful gazebo from her patio.

When she reached the gazebo she ordinarily turned around and walked the other direction to the far end of the path on her side of the lake. This morning was no different. She walked at her steady gait to the far end, where other neighbors on her side of the lake had installed a covered boat dock with boat slips and an attached fishing pier. She didn't think the boathouse and pier were really very nicely done. She always thought that when the day came for it to be rebuilt, she'd pay for it so it could be done properly.

This morning, as she approached the dock and pier, she became aware of an unpleasant odor. Her first thought was that some thoughtless neighbor had abandoned a bucket of fish nearby. She decided to keep on with her walk, which was through the boathouse structure then to the end of the fishing pier culminating in an about-face and return to her home. This morning she found the environment of the boathouse and pier had an intruder.

Sitting in the covered boathouse, on the edge of an empty boat slip, was a disheveled middle-aged man. As she walked by that slip, she knew he was the source of the fish bucket smell. He glared at her as she passed. She glared back.

As she continued to the end of the pier, she tried to think if he was one of the neighbors. Not hardly, she concluded. Then it hit her like a bolt of lightning. He was a homeless man. Was he setting up camp on her side of the lake? Should she notify the authorities? Should she give him money? Clothes? She still had a couple of boxes of her dead husband's clothes in the attic.

The intruder looked and smelled dirty and very poor when she'd walked by him. She decided to take a closer look at him on her return lap.

She slowed her walk from the end of the pier so it wouldn't look like she was slowing only when passing by him. As she got close to him she planned to take an inventory of his appearance. When she was very near him, he reached in his ratty jacket and pulled out a package of cigarettes. He removed one from the pack, tore the filter off and tossed it on the floor of the dock, directly in her path. He then lit the cigarette. Once again he glared at her as she passed by, casually exhaling smoke her direction.

What the?! She was outraged. She picked up her pace and walked back to her home. She sat on her patio for a long time. How did he afford a pack of cigarettes? Didn't they cost ten dollars a pack, or more, these days? What nerve to litter on her side of the lake! What was her next move? She had to formulate a plan. She